"What is it, angel?" he said, his words more demanding than they had any right to be.

He should walk away, his gut said. Leave her to her mysterious problem. It was none of his concern. Nothing could come of further entangling himself with her. Especially now that Simon knew that she was not some nobody who would disappear into the night as she'd hinted. Now that he knew she was a mainstay of the industry with all her connections and her successful career.

She was Anya Raawal, the sister of the powerful and, by her own admission, overly protective Raawal brothers.

One scandalous escapade, one forbidden encounter, was more than enough.

He moved toward her, giving her enough time to slip away.

Her fingers tightened over the sill behind her, her face turning up toward him in challenge.

He reached her but didn't touch her. Just being near her, breathing in the scent of her, made his skin hum. He knew she felt the instant pull too in how her eyes widened. The fever that was already beginning to demand that he taste her lips just once more. "What did you give up all those years ago?"

Tara Pammi can't remember a moment when she wasn't lost in a book—especially a romance, which was much more exciting than a mathematics textbook at school. Years later, Tara's wild imagination and love for the written word revealed what she really wanted to do. Now she pairs alpha males who think they know everything with strong women who knock that theory and them off their feet!

Books by Tara Pammi

Harlequin Presents

Returning for His Unknown Son

Born into Bollywood

Claiming His Bollywood Cinderella
The Surprise Bollywood Baby

Once Upon a Temptation

The Flaw in His Marriage Plan

Signed, Sealed...Seduced

The Playboy's "I Do" Deal

Visit the Author Profile page
at Harlequin.com for more titles.

Tara Pammi

THE SECRET SHE KEPT IN BOLLYWOOD

HARLEQUIN

PRESENTS

Recycling programs for this product may not exist in your area.

ISBN-13: 978-1-335-56870-0

The Secret She Kept in Bollywood

Harlequin Enterprises ULC
22 Adelaide St. West, 41st Floor
Toronto, Ontario M5H 4E3, Canada
www.Harlequin.com

Printed in U.S.A.

THE SECRET SHE KEPT
IN BOLLYWOOD

CHAPTER ONE

SOMETHING MOMENTOUS will happen today. Follow your heart bravely. Anya Raawal stepped out of the car, the little line from her favorite astrology app running circles in her mind. From the moment she'd opened her eyes this morning, Anya had felt the change in the energy around her. Even her quick call to the astrology pundit she consulted with every month had shown that Saturn was leaving some part of her chart and was going to grant her a departing boon.

Several years of tormenting her with health issues and the loss of her beloved grandmother—who'd been more of a parent to her than her real ones—and the cranky universe was apparently going to give her a gift.

Anya was *so* ready for it—whether that was a new creative challenge that would push her to her limits, an old friend walking back into her life or she'd even settle for Mama finding a new hobby that would stop her from trying to set up Anya with yet another "perfect" man.

Sighing, she gestured at Salim Bhai to drive off. A major problem with having staff who had seen you skin your knees and soothed the bumps with Band-Aids and hugs was that they all saw far too much of things she wanted to keep private.

She didn't mind their concern, for the most part. To be honest, she was more than grateful for the staff who had more than once stepped in as caring, concerned adults when her famous movie-star parents had been far too busy with their very messed-up, mostly public, marital dramas and ego wars.

It had been Salim Bhai's wife Noor, and Anya's grandmother who'd nursed Anya back to health from a serious case of blood loss after giving birth to a baby girl at eighteen and from the spiral of depression she'd gone into after giving her up for adoption.

But today, she couldn't stand the extra scrutiny. Nor for them or any of her family to mock her for her beliefs.

She walked up the steps of the luxury five-star hotel where the rehearsals were happening for their production company Raawal House of Cinema's next blockbuster. Her brother Virat was a critically acclaimed director but also often a beast on set.

Now, with his wife Zara, back to work after giving birth to their son, rumors were that his rudeness had reached new heights. So there was no reason for Anya to be here today.

As the head costume designer for the period movie, she wouldn't be needed at the rehearsals. But it was as if there was hook in her belly, pulling her toward this meeting. She knew she was being even more eccentric than usual. That her deep belief in all things cosmic bothered her eldest brother Vikram, to no end.

But it was her chosen madness, her comfort blanket, and she was loath to give it up. It wasn't that she waited for some kind of sign from the stars, but that she believed in listening to the universe.

She breezed in through the front doors and took the lift, refusing to be thwarted by the idea of her bossy, overprotective older brothers focusing their unwanted attention on her. Hopefully, their respective wives—God, how she adored her two sisters-in-law, Naina and Zara—would tell her two big brothers to stick their big noses out of Anya's business.

The security in the lobby of the twenty-second floor waved her in. Anya ducked into one suite after another, absorbing the energy of the room and then walking out when it didn't resonate with her. There was something here…she could feel it thrumming through her veins.

She walked into the biggest suite on the floor to find her brothers, Vikram and Virat, and her sister-in-law Zara and a number of other team members.

A small makeshift dais had been created out of the raised sitting area.

Anya waved at her sister-in-law, who'd looked up from the script when the girl on the stage caught her attention. The movie was about a warrior queen that Zara would be playing, and the younger girl had been cast as the teen version of the queen. While Anya hadn't met the young actress chosen for the role, she'd already started researching the time period and had begun sketching out her wardrobe. Sooner or later, she'd meet her. Especially since both her brothers had sung the praises of the girl's natural talent on stage.

Her name was Meera Verma—daughter of the now-late Rani Verma, one of the most celebrated actresses of Bollywood more than a decade ago. The actress had retired from Bollywood and public life to raise a family and had never returned.

The girl was reading lines from the script in her hand, her voice deep and loud, her plump face illuminated by the overhead lights.

Anya walked closer to the stage, her heart racing so fast that she could hear the echo of it in her entire body. Even thirteen years later, she couldn't forget that beautiful face. Those large distinctive light brown eyes—catlike eyes of the man that had fathered Anya's child—were almost too big for her round face. And then there were the wide pink lips and the dark little finger-width mole that made a slash through the girl's left eyebrow…the one imperfection in her baby's face which had only made her even more perfect in Anya's eyes.

The very baby girl that she'd given up thirteen years ago, the baby she hadn't been strong enough to look after—not mentally, not physically—the baby who'd stolen a piece of her heart in the couple of hours that she'd been held in her mother's arms…this young actress was her daughter.

Meera… The girl's name was Meera… Her daughter's name was Meera.

That's what the universe had brought her here for?

To show her the baby that had been a piece of her heart all grown up?

To dangle the girl in front of Anya when she couldn't be a part of her life, when she couldn't claim any kind of relationship with her?

To make Anya's torment that she had struggled with for thirteen years, even more sharp and painful?

A huge sob built through her chest, sucking out all her breath, leaving her shaking.

Somehow, Anya managed to walk out of the large sitting room, her eyes full of unshed tears, careful to not catch any of her family's eyes.

Her heart breaking all over again…even after all these years.

Simon De Acosta was not a fan of the movie industry and everything it entailed. He'd seen firsthand the high accolades and the low reviews and broken contracts and nepotism at play and the wreckage it had created within the fragile but brilliant mind of his wife Rani. He would never forget the number of years she'd paid her dues in minor roles, forever trying to stay on the right side of powerful men who pulled all the strings.

After several years, Rani's perseverance had finally borne fruit and she'd reached the heights of fame even she'd only dreamed of. But by then, it had done indelible harm to not only to their marriage but also her mental and physical health. Their failure to conceive had broken her down even more.

The only saving grace had been the arrival of Meera in their lives—she'd wrought the miracle that Simon had tried to achieve for years. At only a day old, Meera had gotten her mother to slow down. At a month old, she'd gotten Rani to quit the long hours and the brutal pace—even though her career had been at its peak—and retire.

No lifestyle where she disappeared for weeks on a shoot and he also traveled internationally for work would work for her precious baby girl, Rani had announced with that focused fixation that had often unnerved Simon. But he'd been more than happy to go along with her decision. With his real estate business at a place where he could dictate his own lifestyle, they'd moved to Singapore immediately. Even their marriage had had a second life breathed into it after years of conflict created by two ambitious, demanding careers and the strife and pain caused by their failure to conceive a child.

Until Rani's restlessness had begun once more three years ago and things had begun to fall apart. All over again.

And now, eighteen months after losing Rani in a car crash, he was back in the city of Mumbai with Meera in tow. He'd done his best to persuade Meera to turn away from Bollywood but acting was in her blood, just as it had been in Rani's. It didn't matter that she was adopted.

Simon rubbed a hand over his face and stepped out of the lift into the expansive lobby. It seemed like he'd only blinked twice, and in that time not only had Meera been scouted at a shopping mall of all places, but the acclaimed director Virat Raawal himself had given her a screen test and called her his next incredible find.

Since losing Rani, it was the first time Simon had seen Meera excited about something. Neither had he been able to argue with his thirteen-year-old daughter's wisdom that without her mom, their home was not a home anymore, nor were they any more than automatons surviving each bleak, empty day.

He'd been so wrapped up in his guilt and grief—two emotions that fed each other—that he hadn't even noticed that Meera's grades had been suffering or that she'd retreated from a vibrant social life.

This was a good move, he reminded himself now. It wasn't healthy for him or Meera to be so…isolated as they'd been the last eighteen months. Now, he just needed to find someone trustworthy to watch over Meera for the next few months during the preproduction and the shoot, especially when he traveled for work.

He'd already interviewed several agencies but Meera, being thirteen, hated almost every one of the candidates they'd met. His wife had raised Meera to be not only a well-adjusted, independent girl but also confident in her own decision-making.

For the next few weeks, though, Simon was determined to spend every spare minute their schedules afforded with Meera. He checked his watch. It was six in the evening, which meant Meera wouldn't finish for another hour at least. But he would hang around. He needed to get to know all the members of the production team despite his irrational aversion for the industry. Even the powerful Raawal brothers of whom everyone sang litanies of praise.

Simon was about to walk into the rehearsal suite when he saw a woman kneeling on the floor in the small circular lobby tucked at the end of the corridor.

With Mumbai's skyline visible through the high glass windows, her long neck and slender back were clearly delineated. A faint light spilled into the small sitting area hidden from the view of the long corridor that opened into the various suites. Her shoulders were shaking, her head bowed as if weighed down by insurmountable grief.

Should he walk away?

Rani used to tease him mercilessly for his unmodern instinct to help damsels in distress. But he couldn't just…ignore the woman, could he? Especially now, when he was the father of a teenage girl and had to hope that someone would show her a kindness if she needed it, under any circumstance.

Stopping at a short distance from her, Simon crouched down with one hand on the sofa behind him. "Miss, is everything okay?" he whispered, trying to make his broad form shrink into something less threatening. Which was nearly impossible.

The woman raised her head, her gaze full of shock and…grief. Grief that he'd seen in his own reflection far too much these past eighteen months and recognized only too well.

The woman was young, barely late twenties maybe. Large brown eyes, followed by a distinctive nose that was too big for her face and a wide mouth…not classically beautiful like Rani had been. But the strong, stark lines of her face and the stubborn resolve to her pointed chin tugged at him.

He didn't dare look below her neck for something about her was ringing all the bells in his body, waking up a hunger that had been choked by grief and guilt even before Rani had died.

Despite the warning, his greedy senses nonetheless registered the smooth expanse of golden-brown skin left bare by the deep square neck of the woman's white top. Thin lace shimmered at the neckline kissing the upper swells of her breasts. She was tall and slender and yet curvy in all the right places—voluptuous. Her hair was jet-black with golden highlights in it, cut stylishly to frame her face. The silky ends moved with her baby-bird-like movements as she tilted her head.

What the hell was wrong with him?

The last thing the woman needed was a forty-three-year-old man to be checking her out while she was in the middle of what was clearly a panic attack. Simon exhaled roughly, willing his traitorous body to calm down. And yet he couldn't help but enjoy the slow hum of attraction simmering beneath his skin. It had been so long since he'd felt anything like it.

Tears had drawn rivulets over her sharp cheekbones and pooled around her mouth. She stared at him and yet, Simon knew she hadn't really registered his presence. There was a blankness in her eyes that terrified him to his bones.

"Hey, I'm Simon," he said in a soft, steady voice. "Are you in pain? Should I call for a doctor?"

The woman shook her head. A fat tear dropped to her chin and disappeared down her neck and into the blouse.

"Okay, that's good," he said, settling onto his knees, keeping his hands on his thighs where she could see them. "I'll just sit here for a while with you, yeah?"

She didn't nod but he saw her shoulders relax.

He waited like that for a few minutes before prompting, "Is there anyone I can call for you? A family member?"

She shook her head very emphatically at the last. Was she in danger from them? His blood roared at the very idea. "Okay. That's okay."

Slowly, she scrubbed a hand over her face.

Simon braced himself for her to walk away. He was after all a total stranger. And yes, he had to brace himself because suddenly he didn't want her to leave. Not until he spent a little more time in her company while she pulled herself together.

"Whatever help or comfort you need, big or small, I'd like to help. Whenever you're ready, that is," he added.

"Can you turn back time?" she said at last, in a voice turned husky by her tears.

Her question struck him deep in his heart, pricking the guilt button, reminding him of how helpless he'd felt faced with Rani's dissatisfaction with their life together. It didn't matter that Rani and he had fallen out of love with one another in the last few years. She'd been a part of his life—his best friend, his investor, his lover—for more than two decades. Her loss was raw and real. He settled back against the sofa, his fingers steepled on top of his knees. "That's a question I've asked myself so many times. But all the wealth and power in the world can't help anyone to do that."

She scrubbed her hand over her face once again and mirrored his pose against the coffee table. Their feet sat parallel, almost touching—his booted and hers pink toed and sandaled—as did their knees. It was impossible to not notice her long legs and toned thighs bared by dark denim shorts. Or her smooth golden-brown skin. Or that her every moment, every turn of her head, every lift of her limb was imbued with a languid grace.

"It's a stupid question, isn't it?" she scoffed. "We assume that if we can go back into the past, we'd make different decisions." She inhaled sharply and her mouth stretched in a watery smile. "But the truth is we can't make different decisions." She looked at her laced fingers, and then looked up. "At least I wouldn't have. Couldn't have. But I still revisit it as if I had different choices."

Simon leaned his head against the sofa and closed his eyes. He knew exactly what she meant. The last, bitter fight he and Rani had engaged in still kept him up most nights.

Her solution to breathing new life into their marriage, to restore her increasing dissociation from him and Meera had been to suggest they try to conceive through another round of IVF again.

It had been unacceptable to him.

Maybe she'd forgotten what trauma she'd put her body and heart through the last time, but he hadn't.

Even his argument that she was nearly forty and that kind of stress on her body might send her mental health into decline like the last time hadn't helped. His refusal and her pushing that it was the only solution had festered and blazed and grown like a resentful wound until it had burst into a bitter, hateful fight the very night she had stormed out and then died in a car accident.

Could he have changed anything about the last few years of his marriage with Rani? When Meera and he hadn't been enough for her? What if he had agreed to her plea to try IVF again, even though it hadn't worked when she'd been much younger and had nearly been the end of them? What if they hadn't argued that last day so bitterly before she'd driven off? Would she still be alive today?

Those questions tormented him almost every waking moment.

"Nothing will ever," he said, opening his eyes and coming back to the present, "stop us from wishing we could act differently." He exhaled. "There's only striving for acceptance for the choices that have been already made."

She lifted her lashes and met his gaze properly this time. As if she was finally seeing him—this stranger, a man who'd stopped to chat with her. Noticing things about him. Listening to the pain behind his words. "You understand," she said simply.

He gave her a simple nod. Despite the heavy tone of their musings, Simon noted her sudden alertness as she watched him. The stifled gasp as she became aware of him.

Still, her gaze swept over him, quick and greedy and heated, just as his had done earlier. A bare few seconds but he felt it all the same. Maybe because of the artlessness of it. Maybe because she wore her shock at her reaction to him so openly on her face. He could almost pinpoint the moment her mind registered the darkly potent electricity arcing between them. Her knees shifted in a jerky move, as if to get away from him, but boxed in between the coffee table and the sofa, her long legs fell back against his. Even with his trouser-covered legs, Simon felt the weight of them like a shock to his system.

Long, thick lashes flicked down in shyness but that stubbornness he'd noted in her chin brought them back up. Simon could see the very second she decided she wouldn't let grief win. Saw her wonder if she could use their mutual attraction to dig herself out of whatever had brought her to her knees.

Watching her fight the shadows of her grief was sexy as hell. Every muscle in his body tightened in an instantaneous reaction. The urge to stay here, the urge to do more than talk was…so strong that he fisted his hands at his sides.

"I'm… Angel," she said, stretching out a hand over their touching knees. The echo of tears was still in her voice but there was also a raspy huskiness now.

"Simon," he said automatically, not reaching out to take her hand.

If he thought she'd be hurt by his reluctance to touch her, she proved him wrong. She simply kept her hand there, a brow raising in her beautiful face, throwing down a gauntlet. Calling him on his sudden aloofness.

Hell, he was a forty-three-year-old man and he was scared of touching this fragile beauty? Was he that dead inside?

Simon took her hand in his, and felt the jolt go up his arm, and all the way down through his body to his groin. Her fingers were soft and slender but full of calluses. He rubbed the bridge of her thumb with the pad of his, marveling at how deliciously good even the simple contact felt. How life-affirming. He wanted to touch her more, everywhere, wanted to smooth out the furrow between her brows with his thumb, wanted to bury his mouth in the sensitive crook of her neck and shoulders.

Her light brown eyes widened, her nostrils flaring with an indrawn breath.

He dropped her hand, the contact igniting a fire inside him he knew he couldn't quench. "If you don't need anything else—"

"Thank you for your kindness," she said, her voice suddenly dripping with a formality he disliked immensely. Even though he'd forced her to it with his own withdrawal. "I should go. Before someone sees me."

"It was nothing," he said, at a loss for words. All the questions he wanted to ask were too intrusive. All the things he wanted to say to her…didn't bear thinking, much less saying out loud. Not with their adult-rated content.

One hand on the sofa behind her, she quickly pushed

up to her feet and Simon followed. To find her swaying on her feet, her skin pale and drawn tight.

He clamped his hands over her shoulders, frowning. "You're not all right."

She pushed away from his hold, her eyes on his mouth. "I just stood up too fast and I haven't eaten anything all day."

He scowled. Even as every inch of him was aware of her body, her movements, her expressions. She was tall and slender and yet curvy at her breasts and hips. Vulnerable clearly but also strong. "It's six thirty in the evening."

She bit her lower lip. "I had other things on my mind. More important things."

"Let me take you to dinner then," he said, the offer bursting out of him before he thought it through. This woman was dangerous to his peace and yet, he wanted her company for just a little while longer. "Let me take care of you."

"I don't need another man to tell me I need looking after. I have enough of those in my life. I need…" She tugged at the strap of the cross-body bag that fell between her breasts, making them more pronounced. "I should go. Thanks for…everything."

He should've let her go then. Instead he clasped his fingers over her wrist in a gentle movement, contrary to how his pulse zigzagged almost violently through him. "What do you need, Angel?"

Suddenly, she stood close, her front to his side, almost grazing him. Almost…but not quite. She was only a couple of inches shorter than him, so her breath hit him on his jaw, her gaze sliding to his mouth and then upward in a blatant gesture. "Someone who'll listen to what I say *I* need. Someone who'll give me what I need." She stared into his eyes, challenge glinting there. In seconds, that naive fragility had transformed into pure temptation with a spine of steel. A scornful smile split her mouth. "It's not you though. I can already tell you're one of those men who doesn't really see me. You're someone who loves playing the knight, someone who deals in honor and duty but doesn't really like getting his hands dirty."

God, the woman had his number down perfect. Hadn't Rani been just as resentful of him that he wouldn't give her what she wanted? Hadn't he tormented himself wondering if he should've just given in, even when he'd known it would end in total disaster?

Was she right that he'd refused Rani because he hadn't the emotional energy to love her as she needed to be loved? Because he'd simply assumed that he knew better?

That this stranger could pierce him so easily, that she challenged what he'd assumed was honor grated like the scrape of nails. "You don't know what I can do for you," he said, his voice low and deep and far too commanding to use on a woman he'd found in distress. A stranger, at that.

There was no doubt that he was temporarily out of his mind.

And yet…she didn't look at him as if he was losing his mind. As if he was being a creepy stranger hitting on the woman he'd found in tears. As if his sudden demand for her to let him in, to let him do something for her was anything but...utter madness.

"Ask me," he said, his blood full of a deafening hum, his heart punching away at his rib cage as if it had just stuttered back to glorious life.

"Anything?" she said sensually, turning toward him.

Simon cast one look at the closed door of the rehearsal suite and nodded. Reaching for his hand, she laced her fingers around his. Clinging to him, certainly but also full of resolve. And then she dragged him after her—this woman, this stranger he'd met no more than twenty minutes ago—and he followed.

He knew what she wanted. It was irresponsible and scandalous and reckless and... But it was also like coming awake after decades of slumber.

It was being alive for a moment in time, knowing that the future was nothing but a long stretch of emptiness and silence. Nothing but guilt and grief ravaging him. And Simon decided he wanted this moment. After three years of struggling with Rani's restlessness and disillusion with the life they'd built, after months of loneliness even when she was lying next to him, after the hollow powerlessness of not being able to give her what she demanded, this woman's naked desire for him was a soothing benediction he hadn't known he'd needed.

A stringent reminder of his own wants and needs.

A much-needed human connection.

He would indulge her and he would gorge himself by giving her whatever she wanted.

CHAPTER TWO

IT WAS NOTHING but sheer madness.

Her brothers were behind a closed door not a few hundred feet away. Her daughter…one she couldn't claim, one she couldn't hold and touch and love openly, not in this lifetime, was also behind that same door. The very thought threatened to bring Anya to her knees again.

And she was dragging a stranger—a man who'd shown her only kindness—along with her into all this crazy. This reckless woman wasn't her.

But if she didn't do this, if she didn't take what he offered, if she didn't grasp this thing between them and hold on to it, it felt like she'd stay on her knees, raging at a fate she couldn't change, forever… And Anya refused to be that woman anymore.

It was as if she was walking through one of those fantastical daydreams she still had sometimes when her anxiety became too much. The one where she just spun herself into an alternate world because in actual reality she was nothing but a coward.

Now, those realities were merging, and the possibility that she could be more than her grief and guilt and loss was the only thing that kept her standing upright. It took her a minute to find an empty suite, to turn the knob and then lock it behind them.

Silence and almost total darkness cloaked them. A sliver of light from the bathroom showed that it was another expansive suite, and they were standing in the entryway. Anya pressed herself against the door with the man facing her. The commanding bridge of his nose that seemed to slash through his face with perfect symmetry, the square jaw and the broad shoulders...the faint outline of his strong, masculine features guided her. But those eyes...wide and penetrating, full of an aching pain and naked desire that could span the width of an ocean...she couldn't see those properly anymore. Without meeting those eyes, she could pretend this was a simple case of lust.

Simon, she said in her mind, tasting his name there first...so tall and broad that even standing at five-ten, she felt so utterly encompassed by him.

Simon with the kind eyes and the tight mouth and a fleck of gray at his temples. And a banked desire he'd been determined to not let drive him.

But despite that obvious struggle, he was here with her. Ready to give her whatever she wanted from him.

What did she want? How far was she going to take this temporary madness?

His arm lifted, his hand moving toward the light switch next to her head. Anya captured it with her own and his big hand encompassed hers. The contact sent a jolt through her, the rough scrape of his palm, the tight grip of his fingers a lifeline she couldn't let go.

"Don't," she whispered, all her courage deserting her as fast as it had come, leaving her cold and shivering.

Her knees shook and he moved closer, his hands on her arms gently holding her up. "It's okay, Angel," he said, in that deep, bass voice that resonated through her body. "You're okay."

Anya bent her head and found his shoulder. Slowly, she nuzzled her way across to his throat, and tried to breathe. His fingers instantly moved to her neck, wrapping around her nape, tethering her in the here and now, while she hyperventilated.

"I've never done anything like this before," she offered lamely. Letting the real world intrude in here too, allowing rationality and common sense and all kinds of noise back into her head. But none of those could save her from the pain. Nor even offer comfort. Only he could, only this could…

A bark of a laugh fell from his mouth—more self-deprecating than anything else. "And you still don't have to do anything you don't want to, Angel. Nothing matters other than this moment—not the past, not the future."

She breathed in deep and the most decadent scent—his skin and cologne—filled her lungs. That lick of desire flared again, cutting through the loop of thoughts her mind wanted to drown her in.

Awareness inched back into her body, his rock-hard thighs anchoring her when she let herself sway forward, the heat of his body cutting through the chill pervading her skin, the warmth of his breath coating her forehead, tickling the hairs at her temple…her body coming alive in a way she hadn't known in so long. "There's only now," she said, her resolve coming back.

The pad of his thumb found the sensitive hollow of her jaw below her ear. "Yes." One long finger pressed against her pulse, his touch shifting from tender and protective to something darker and demanding and… possessive. "Now, will you tell me what you truly want, Angel? We're alone in the dark and I have nothing to guide me but your words. Nothing to guide my actions but your wishes. There's no honor, no duty, no playing the hero. I'm here to do your bidding."

Heat flushed through every inch of Anya's skin at how easily he'd transformed from a kind stranger to this…seductive man. At the delicious promise in his words. At the easy way he'd made this all about her.

Lifting her head, she inched her hands toward him. They landed somewhere below his chest. Slowly, she sent them up his torso, loving the taut, muscular feel of him under her fingers, relishing the strong thud of his heart, and then she clasped her fingers at the nape of his neck.

The ends of his silky hair tickled the tips of her fingers. Stretching up on tiptoe, she leaned in until her mouth found his jaw—stubbled and rough and oh so delicious against her lips. "I want you. Everything you can give me, everything you want from me. I want us both satisfied and limp and incapable of thought."

"Everything I can give?"

"Yes, Simon."

She loved his name on her lips. She loved the sense of freedom it gave her, the curl of feminine power his groan sent through her lower belly as she articulated every dark thought that had bloomed into life the moment her eyes had met his. "I want to forget what I gave up. I want to forget how empty my life feels if I let that loss take over. I'm sure you think I'm being hysterical."

His hand covered her mouth. "I don't. The moment I looked into your eyes, the moment I saw your grief, I saw myself. I know exactly what you mean, Angel. I've mourned too."

Anya kissed his palm. "Then indulge us both. I want to feel alive. I want nothing but pleasure."

His mouth found hers with another searing groan.

A blinding wave of need blazed into life in every pore at the contact. All the scenarios she'd played out in her head in the span of a few seconds, all the suppositions and assumptions she'd made about this sudden attraction…everything turned to dust, everything left behind by the instant, consuming heat of his touch.

Her body slammed into his. She moaned as her breasts, already heavy and begging to be touched, flattened against the hard breadth of his chest. His fingers around her neck tightened as he nipped at her lower lip, demanding access.

Anya opened up obediently and then he was licking into her mouth with a demanding eagerness that dialed up her own hunger. They kissed as if this was their last kiss, not their first. As if they already knew each other's darkest desires. As if they knew how to give what the other needed and demanded without restraint or shame.

His other palm kneaded her hip, pressing long fingers into her willing flesh. Then he moved them up her sides, stroking, learning, tracing, inflaming her while his mouth soothed and licked and laved.

When he left her mouth for a much-needed breath, Anya sank her fingers into his hair and pulled him back. Out of pure, clawing instinct to be closer to him, she lifted her leg and wrapped it around his hip. His hand was at her thigh instantly, holding her up, and then he brought his lower body against hers. Her sex clenched deep and hard at the flutter of his fingers at her inner thigh.

The urgent press of his erection against her groin made a curse rip out of her mouth so filthy that Anya saw the flash of his white grin in the darkness. So full of wicked want that she thrust up against him in a mindless search for more. It was as instinctual as breathing, this need to rile him up into the same frenzy, to drive him toward the edge where she was ready to free-fall. The next time her hips met his, she stayed there, relishing the hard length of him against her lower belly, reveling in the raw proof of what she did to him.

It was his turn to color the air around them and he did it in such explicit detail that Anya blushed far more than from anything they'd done so far.

Her back slammed into the door behind her but somehow he had his palm pressed up between the door and her back before she could be hurt. He was everywhere—in her mouth, on her skin, curling into a deep want in her very muscles.

"I can keep kissing you like this until the night comes to an end," he said, licking a languorous path over the shell of her ear, kissing his way across her jaw to her mouth, every hard contour of his body pressed up against her.

"More. I need more."

She felt his smile against her mouth and it was the most sensuous thing Anya had ever experienced. Dampness gushed between her thighs and she moaned, wanting his fingers there. Wanting whatever he'd give her there.

He pulled away from her, the rhythm of his breaths shallow. "I found you falling apart not that long ago. I don't want to take advantage of you, Angel."

"I thought you weren't playing the knight anymore."

His mouth quirked up on one side, his fingers tracing her sensitive lips. "It's called simple decency."

"And if I tell you that I need this? That I don't want the past to be the only thing that defines me, that I'm making my pleasure a choice? You could leave me feeling worse than before." She lifted his hand to her mouth and kissed the rough palm. Then she brought it down her neck to her breast. "Or you could see this all the way through," she said, pure resolve and naked need in her tone.

His fingers cupped her breast, kneading, teasing, making her breath come in short pants. She arched into his touch, her spine all but melted desire. "As you promised."

"I will stop the moment you change your mind."

"Don't stop, Simon."

"As you wish, Angel."

The pop-pop of her buttons as he ripped more than a couple made her shiver with anticipation. Clever fingers pulled down the flimsy lacy cup of her bra and then his bare hand covered her breast. "Protection," he whispered, even as his fingers drew mindless circles around the taut nipple begging for his attention.

"Condom in my bag," she murmured, writhing against his clever fingers, a damp flush coating her skin. Moaning, she arched into his touch. "More."

That's all she had to say. In the next breath, his mouth was at her breast.

Anya let out a long, deep groan that seemed to be ripped from the depths of her as he played with her nipple using the tip of his tongue and then drew it into his mouth.

On and on, switching between both breasts, until she was writhing against his body, and crying out. "I won't be of any use to you if you continue like this," she warned, her voice ragged.

He took her mouth in a slow, soft kiss this time, his hands deserting her breasts to move down. His fingers fluttered over the small curve of her belly to the seam of her denim shorts. "That's the point of this. I don't want you to do anything but enjoy this. All I want is for you to tell me what you want."

"I want it all," Anya said, hiding her face in the warm crook of his neck.

His fingers undid the button and the zipper of her

shorts and then slowly, oh so slowly that she could hear the roar of her heart in her ears, he sneaked them in. Ever so gently, he traced the lips of her sex.

Anya licked the hollow of his throat, and nipped at his skin, begging silently with her own caresses.

And then his tongue thrust into her mouth in an erotic kiss as he drew her shorts and panties down her hips. They dropped to her ankles and she carefully stepped out of them. "Damn, you're wet for me."

Anya flushed, loving the rough texture of his words even more than the smooth caresses of his fingers, learning every inch of her sex. "Widen your legs," he whispered at her ear and she did. "More?"

"God, yes."

One long finger thrust into her and then two all the while his thumb played at her sensitive bud. Anya banged her head against the door, release hovering at the edge of her skin, shimmering just out of reach.

She had been here at this point, so many times, frustrated beyond measure at not pushing off, her body so desperately craving the release. She'd stopped trying when she'd realized she needed a sense of intimacy with someone else in order to climax but that was the very thing that scared her. And now…now she was here with Simon and all she wanted was to lose herself in the pleasure he was giving her.

She thrust her hips in tune to his fingers' play, chasing them mindlessly but her climax stayed out of her reach, sending frustrated tears to the back of her eyes.

A groan left her mouth as the peak started slipping away.

His lips were at her temple, instantly soothing, brushing so gently that she wanted to burrow into him. "Shh… Angel, it's okay." He flicked at the damp tendrils sticking to her forehead, his breath ghosting over her skin like a cool caress. "What do you need? Whatever you need…it's yours." He didn't say it arrogantly, but with such a stark promise in his voice that Anya opened her eyes.

The darkness was no barrier with the way he looked at her, the way he devoured every nuance of her expression.

"I don't know," she whispered, shedding the last layer of vulnerability, stripping herself completely bare.

No one had seen her like this. No one had ever known her like this. There was strength and power and a bone-deep pleasure in giving this to him in a corner of darkness, this man who'd seen her at her lowest and cared enough to stay. When he simply stared at her with that infinite patience he seemed to have, she bit her lip. "I don't… I don't have a lot of experience with men. Or achieving orgasms."

He licked the tip of her mouth, a wink and a smile flashing at her. The smile was wide and wicked, and Anya had never thought a smile could taste like such pure acceptance and unfettered joy.

Counterpoint to that smile, his finger curled deep inside her, hitting a point so deep and pleasurable that she cried out in ecstasy. It was unlike anything she'd felt before, the barrage of pressure and pleasure that coiled there. "That's not a problem." His mouth was against hers again, lazily sipping, licking, his other hand stroking over her neck. "Because it means we get to try so many things. Where are you most sensitive?"

Anya cupped her breasts even as fiery heat coated her cheeks at the dark satisfaction in his eyes. But there was no space for modesty or shyness here, no space for shame. Only pleasure.

"Ahh…my favorite too," he said with a roguish smile and then his mouth fluttered down from her pulse, nipping the slope of her breast so that the tiny bite of pain made the pleasure of his fingers moving inside her that much sharper and delicious and then his tongue was at her nipple again.

"I love how lushly you fit in my palms, how wet you are for me," he said, between licks and nibbles as if she were his favorite sweet. In the dark, Anya saw his wicked eyes glint with satisfaction as he licked his finger. "How sweet you taste to me, Angel. I feel like a randy teenager just imagining how good you'll feel around my shaft…how hungrily you will swallow me whole."

"More words," she said, leaning into him and stretching her thigh higher so that he could go deeper. The ache was building again, faster and more powerful, threatening to shatter her. For the first time in her life, Anya was not afraid. All she wanted was to fragment, to forget, to fly in this moment, be free of the past and the future. "Please, Simon," she whispered, burying her face in his neck and pressing her open mouth against his skin. He tasted like salt and soap and something woodsy and she wanted to devour him whole.

"I love how you reached for this…for me when you

could've simply walked away. I love how you dared me to give you what you want. I love how you pushed me to have this, Angel, have you."

Anya's fingers reached his groin and he let out a deep groan as she traced the outline of his erection with her fingers. But he didn't stop the torment of his fingers or his mouth, building her climb all over again. So well that she was panting when she said, "I want you inside me when I…" Her breath shuddered in and out as once again her release fluttered closer. "Please. This whole thing will shatter once I climax. The real world will intrude…and I'll run away. From you. From myself. I… I need this. I need you inside me. Now."

"Are you sure, Angel?" he asked seriously.

"God, yes. More than anything," Anya answered and with steady fingers, slowly, undid his trousers.

Somehow, they managed to find the condom in her bag. She heard the sound of the package tearing, saw him roll it up his length and then he was kissing her again. With such gentle reverence that she knew she wouldn't forget it for years.

"Tell me one last time what you're thinking," she demanded. "Tell me."

One hand cupped her hip and jerked her away from the main door of the suite toward the wall. Anya flushed, knowing that he was the only one thinking rationally here. And she liked it. She liked being the wild one, the aggressor, the one who took risks and pursued her pleasure boldly. The one who wasn't afraid to trust him and herself, for once.

"I'm thinking this is the most irresponsible thing

I've ever done in my life." A hard kiss to her mouth. "It's also the most alive I've felt in years. You're like a sweet benediction from heaven, an earthly reminder that I'm not dead inside." His fingers at her inner thigh opened her indecently wide. "And I'm never going to live like this again."

Anya felt the head of his erection flicking against her core, and she gasped anew. Sensation zinged and pooled in her lower belly, her entire being stretched taut at the cusp of explosion. The dark was a cover for things she wouldn't have dared ask for in daylight, but the dark also converged every ounce of her being at her sex, damp and ready for him.

"I'm thinking," he continued, feeding himself into her wet heat, inch by tormenting inch, his words a raw whisper at her temple, "that I'll never have another encounter like this." Anya buried her face into his neck at the sharp sting of his invasion. His long fingers on her buttocks, he stilled and waited until she urged him on with a hard kiss. "That I needed this more than I could ever put into words." His voice sounded rough and guttural as he thrust in a little more. "That I'll never meet another woman like you, someone who'll make me this insane." They both groaned when he was lodged all the way inside her. "Someone who'll make me glad that I gave in to temptation for one magical instant."

Hands clenching his rock-hard shoulders, Anya breathed in shallow gasps. Not her imagination, not the one encounter she'd had with Meera's father all of fourteen years ago, nothing had prepared her for the achy fullness that filled her body or the desperate need for release. Her thigh muscles ached at how wide his hips pushed them, her arms burned at how hard she clung to him and that made the pleasure of him inside her that much sweeter.

"You okay, Angel?" he asked, his voice so deep and hoarse that she adored it.

The sharp sting was already receding, and Anya jerked her hips experimentally.

Simon's fingers tightened on her hips, his ragged exhale coating her jaw.

"If it hurts, tell me. We can stop. Now."

She shook her head and searched for his mouth in the darkness. His lips were sweet and soft when she found him. His kiss possessive and alternating with sexy little nips of his teeth. "No…you just…you feel like you're lodged here," she said, dragging his palm to her breast. "I… I'm so very glad to have met you, Simon." He did something with his hips—a swivel and a thrust that made her head bang against the wall, her eyes roll into the back of her head. "And not just because you can do that," she said, giggling.

"I love tasting your smile, Angel," he whispered, mirroring her very thoughts. His hips retreated a fraction before he was pinning hers to the wall again. Anya huffed out a shallow breath, her spine melting. "Now hold on to me, yeah?"

"God, yes."

And then he was thrusting into her hard and fast, while his thumb stubbornly stayed at her clit, applying counterpressure. His mouth was at her neck, his teeth dragging over the sensitive skin there and it was all too much. Anya wrapped her hands around his shoulders and just hung on.

Each thrust against the wall rattled some picture frames she couldn't even see and it only added to the symphony of sounds they made together. He drove her higher and higher, the pressure in her belly tightening.

"You feel amazing, Angel," he groaned, and she swore that with each movement of his body he hit every single pleasure point in hers as if he could weave magic.

Head bowed against his shoulder, Anya came in a sudden rush of such pulsating pleasure that she let out a keening cry. He took that into himself, soothing her and kissing her even as he ravaged her and Anya had never been more aware of, or more in love with her own body than at the moment.

Now that it gave him such pleasure, now that he held it with such reverence. Now that it could send his powerful body shuddering as release crashed into him. His broad shoulders shook as he came with a final thrust that pinioned his hips to hers, his fingers digging into her hips.

Anya hung on, for what felt like eternity, her face buried in his shoulder. But it could have been no more than a few breaths.

"Are you all right?" he asked, his exhale playing with the damp tendrils of her hair sticking to her temples. His chest rose and fell against her, his muscles around her still shuddering from his release.

She nodded, unable to conjure words.

"I'm going to—" she looked up, and his gaze met

hers, steady and reassuring even in the dark that sur-rounded them "—set you to rights, okay? I need to leave soon but we can stay here, like this, for a little longer." He traced the edge of her mouth with a thumb. "Yes, Angel?"

His tenderness threatened to tear her apart. She didn't want him to leave. She wanted to stay in this darkness with him, breathing in the scent of their sex in the air, cocooned in the warmth and secure embrace of his body. "I'm fine," she said, finally. "Do you mind if I leave first? Like I said, I don't want to be found on this floor."

He acknowledged her request with a nod. Slowly, he released his hold on her, his hand moving away from her thigh. When he pulled out of her, Anya drew in a sharp breath at the slight sting. But it had nothing on the emptiness she felt.

He noted her discomfort, this man who seemed to miss nothing, planted a soft kiss on her lips and then righted her clothes with a gentleness that made tears pound at the back of her throat. When he released her from the fortress of the wall and his body, she swayed, her thighs trembling. Instantly, he pulled her toward him until she was leaning into him again.

"I've got you," he said, his hand on her back, his tone tender.

Time passed too swiftly then, and Anya knew she'd get into real trouble—the kind of fuss that her older brothers specialized in—if she didn't get away now. One look at her and they would know everything that had just happened—both the grief that was already inching its way back around her heart and the thoroughly reckless but desperately needed pleasure she'd just indulged in.

With a stranger at that.

With the entire production team two doors away.

She pushed out of his hold and he immediately let her go. Her knuckles tightened around the strap of her bag as if it could somehow steady her fluctuating emotions. Hand on the doorknob, she turned toward him and pressed a soft kiss to his jaw. The stubble tingled her already sensitive lips. "Thank you, Simon, for giving me what I needed. For seeing the real me. I'll never forget…tonight," she amended at the last minute.

And then she was walking through the corridor, into the lift and jumping into a taxi without looking back. She trembled all the way home but there was not a ray of regret inside her for what had happened. Her body ached in a way she wanted to cherish and her smile lingered for a long time even after she let herself into her flat.

Even after she sank into her sheets without having showered, because she wanted to smell Simon and his masculine scent all over her skin for a few more hours.

Today, she'd lived a little.

Today, she'd carved a moment's happiness for herself.

Today, she'd trusted herself and the universe and she vowed to try to be a little braver every day.

CHAPTER THREE

ANYA HID OVER the next three days.

Not licking her wounds in private so much as bracing herself for the next time she'd run into…her daughter. The next time when she couldn't simply run away, but would have to chat with her as if she were any other actress for whom Anya was designing a wardrobe.

For a hot minute, she considered telling her brother Virat that she had to drop out of this project. He wouldn't like it one bit—his creative vision and hers clicked so well usually—but he'd respect her wishes.

But for one thing, it would bring all of her family's scrutiny down on her head. Despite the passive-aggressive dynamics of her brothers' relationship with their parents, in this one thing, they all seemed to agree unanimously. That Anya must be protected, even if it meant invading her privacy and trashing the boundaries she'd tried very hard to set with her interfering family.

And for another thing, how long would she hide? What if Meera became a staple of the industry? How could she bear to lose the little time she had to get to know the girl who held a piece of her heart?

The fourth evening, she arrived at the bungalow that had once belonged to her grandparents. Now it was the home of her brother Virat and his wife Zara, where Zara was throwing a small, intimate party.

She'd show her face, play with her toddler nephew and her infant niece, chat with her other sister-in-law, Naina, about the screenplay she was working on, smile at her parents, hug her brothers and leave.

The first half hour of the party, Anya did just that— she caught up with her family and the four close friends Zara had invited. She was even proud of herself— showing her face in polite society as if she were a normally functioning adult, when two unprecedented things had taken place not four days ago in her life.

The last time something like that had happened she'd fallen pregnant at eighteen by a man nine years older than her—a fortune hunter who'd specifically targeted her and then left her when he'd realized he wasn't going to get a slice of the Raawal pie—and she'd retreated into her shell for the next few years. Of course, giving birth, almost dying and then giving up her baby girl had been the most traumatic experiences of her life.

But after the thoroughly scandalous episode she'd indulged in, she felt as if she had finally wrested back some control over her own life. She even felt a little hopeful for her own future.

Lounging on the divan, Anya was laughing at something Vikram and his wife, Naina, said when Meera walked into the sitting lounge.

Dressed in a cotton crop top and high-waisted jeans, her smile so broad that it hurt Anya to look at the girl's face, Meera was palpably excited as she waved at everyone.

Fisting her hands at her sides, Anya fought the urge to run away again. A fake smile pasted to her lips, she forced herself to draw breaths in, counting them in her head. She almost had it together when a dark figure, so broad and tall that Anya blinked, materialized behind Meera.

It was *him*…the stranger who'd given her a slice of paradise.

Who'd belonged to her for a tiny blink of time.

Simon…was here at Zara's party. And he was clearly with Meera.

Why?

A deafening silence descended in her ears, her heart beating a frantic tattoo as Zara walked up to greet Meera and Simon. Through it all, Anya could hear the girl's voice chattering away excitedly.

Papa…she was calling him Papa. Meera was calling him Papa…

The man Anya had had sex with under the cover of darkness, the man she'd poured her heart out to was… Meera's father.

Her baby girl's adoptive father.

God, how had she let this happen? Why was the universe trying to destroy her again?

Anya shot up from the divan, adrenaline pounding through her making flight the only choice left to her. Just as the two of them accompanied by Zara reached her.

"I can't tell you how excited I am to finally meet you, Ms. Raawal," Meera said and Anya stared at her animated face, her throat so tight that it hurt to swallow. "Zara di said you'd come in during the rehearsal, but I must have missed you. I can't tell you what a fan I am of your latest line of clothes for teens." She tugged at the seam of the jeans she was wearing, rocking on the balls of her feet. "Do you know how impossible it usually is for me to find jeans that fit me so well? Just because I'm tall and curvy and…"

"Give Ms. Raawal a chance to respond, Meera," said a deep voice behind the girl. The voice that had whispered the filthiest things in her ear four nights ago.

Heat swarming her cheeks, Anya found her gaze colliding with his. He knew her identity but he didn't reveal it even by the blink of an eyelid.

She should be thankful. She was thankful. But the spiral of her thoughts wouldn't cease… What did he think of her? Would he forbid her from seeing even the little of Meera that she'd hoped for? Would he think her a bad influence?

"I'm Meera De Acosta… Well, Meera Verma for the industry," the girl said, puncturing Anya's spiral. "I'm the daughter of…"

"Rani Verma, I know," Anya said, through numb lips. "I'm excited to meet you too, Ms. Verma. My brother's been singing high praises of you."

"Please, call me Meera. Especially since you're

going to create my wardrobe for the movie and I'm going to pester you a lot."

Anya smiled, despite the spectacular spiral her life was going into. It was impossible to stay unmoved with the girl's adorable smile and easy excitement coming at her in overwhelming waves.

"This is my dad, Simon," Meera said, shifting to the side.

"It's nice to meet you, Ms. Raawal." He sounded as if they'd just met.

She should follow his lead and simply pretend too. Act like it hadn't been a big deal. After all, she was an adult and she hadn't done anything wrong.

But all her warnings and reassurances didn't help.

She stared at his hand stretched out between hers, long fingers with bluntly trimmed nails. Corded wrist with hair sprinkled. That hand had touched her everywhere. Those fingers had pleasured her so intimately. Those powerful thighs had held her against the wall while he... God!

She'd had sex with her daughter's father, had ruined any chances she might have had of being in Meera's life—even temporarily. It was a twist worthy of one of Vikram's blockbuster movies that Virat teased him about so mercilessly.

"Anya?" She heard Zara's voice as if it was coming from far away.

Her vision swam and her breath felt choppy. But before she hit the floor, Simon was there. With his broad shoulders, and concerned eyes, and strong hands holding her tightly.

Their eyes met and Anya saw his concern and his questions.

"I'm okay," she whispered, loath to draw anyone else's attention. Especially her brothers'. "I just need some air."

He nodded and let her go. But not before his jaw hardened and he whispered back, "We're going to talk soon, *Angel*."

This wasn't the kind stranger or the seductive lover. This was a different man—more demanding, terse, even.

Anya pasted a smile onto her lips and turned to Meera. "I'm feeling a little unwell this evening, that's all," she offered, tears prickling at the back of her eyes.

Glad that she'd kept her composure, she walked away. And didn't miss the sensation of Simon's gaze on her back determined to probe to the depths of her soul.

Straightening her spine, Anya made the decision at that moment that she would tell him about Meera. She'd had enough of the damned universe playing games with her.

She was going to tell Simon the truth—for no other reason than that he deserved to know. And because Anya wanted to trust him with the secret she didn't want to carry around alone any longer.

Simon found her on the terrace, her body limned by the moonlight, a couple of hours later. It was ridiculous that he'd spent the last hour chasing her shadow in every corner and nook of the expansive bungalow.

It was ridiculous that he'd barely exchanged any

more than cursory greetings with the Raawal brothers—his entire reason for attending this dinner.

It was ridiculous that he was so concerned about her, a stranger no less, about the stark shock in her eyes when she'd spied him, that he hadn't been able to think of anything else. Ridiculous that he'd left his daughter in the company of Zara and lied that he needed fresh air. Not that Zara had believed it.

But he wanted to talk to his Angel.

Ms. Anya Raawal, he corrected in his head. He'd simply reassure her that he didn't mean her any kind of harm. Make it clear that he had no wish to continue their association. It was a few moments of madness—done with and never to be repeated again. His steps made no sound on the smooth marble floor, but he saw her shoulders tense.

She turned around, her motions jerky, her eyes red rimmed but steadily gazing back at him.

"Are you feeling better now?" he asked, stopping a few feet from her, loathing the very idea of spooking her.

She stared at him, aghast, before she attempted a smile. But he could tell it didn't reach her eyes. It didn't make them sparkle. It didn't remove the stress lines etched around her mouth. "You have to stop asking me that, Simon. Stop…showing me that concern of yours."

"I will, Ms. Raawal," he said formally, and saw her eyes widen. "As soon as you tell me what's wrong with you."

She would say she was fine, and he would nod and that would be that. But she didn't say anything. The silence went on and on, picking up more and more weight until it was nearly unbearable.

For the first time since he'd walked in and seen her, he put his shock and other inconvenient emotions that had been plaguing him aside. Tried to look at the puzzle that was Anya Raawal objectively.

It couldn't be seeing him again that had caused her such shock. When he'd caught sight of her, she'd been sitting on the divan. Her legs folded under her, laughing openly with her family. He hadn't been able to look away. And so he'd seen the laughter turn to shock when she'd spotted Meera. But it was only when she'd seen him behind Meera that it had turned to panic. Just like that day at the hotel.

So what had spooked her then? Again?

"Did someone try to harm you at the hotel? Is that person here today too?"

She didn't laugh at his dramatic conjecture. Her eyes improbably wide, her skin stretched tightly over her cheekbones, she said, "No. Nothing like that."

"Then what is it, Angel?" he said, his words more demanding than they had any right to be. "What keeps sending you into such stark panic? Have you told anyone about it?"

Her chin lifted. "No. Because it's no one else's business but mine," she said with a thread of steel he hadn't heard before.

So there was something then.

He should walk away, his gut said. Leave her to her mysterious problem. It was none of his concern. Nothing could come of further entangling himself with her.

Especially now that he knew that she was not some nobody who would disappear into the night as she'd hinted. Now that he knew she was a mainstay of the industry with all her connections and her successful career.

She was Anya Raawal, the sister of the powerful and, by her own admission, overly protective Raawal brothers. She was also fragile and far too young for him.

One scandalous escapade—one forbidden encounter—was more than enough.

And yet, Simon stood there, caught between his usual common sense and the utter irrationality of wanting to be near her. Of wanting to figure her out. Of wanting to help her. "Not even your brothers?" he taunted.

"Especially not them," she said with just as much vehemence.

He moved toward her, giving her enough time to slip away.

Her fingers tightened over the sill behind her, her face turning up toward him in challenge.

He reached her but didn't touch her. Just being near her, breathing in the scent of her made his skin hum. He knew she felt the instant pull too in how her eyes widened. The madness that was already beginning to demand that he taste her lips just once more. "What did you give up all those years ago?"

"Who were you mourning?" she demanded, tilting her head up to look at him, baring that neck that he wanted to kiss all over again.

"Rani, my wife. She died in a car accident eighteen months ago," he said softly. His guilt dulled right now by the puzzle he was trying to solve. By this woman who upended his thoughts and emotions with her mere presence. "Now you answer my question, Angel. What did you give up?"

Tears pooled in her big eyes and her mouth trembled. "You're not going to like it."

"But you want to tell me," he said, going all in on instinct. He could see it in her face now—this had something to do with him. The inevitability of it had been written on her face the moment she'd seen him tonight and lost all color in her face.

A sudden dread twisted his gut when she didn't deny it. He was about to back off, about to walk away from this woman who'd already made him behave so unlike himself when she looked up at him.

A lone tear fell down her cheek and she wiped it away roughly. "I gave up my baby girl thirteen years ago. I…" She took a deep breath, somehow containing the huge sob that threatened to tear her apart. "I never imagined I'd see her again. I…didn't even realize until I saw her four days ago that she still holds a piece of my heart. That I've been carrying around this love for her here—" she pressed a hand to her chest "—that would create a void in my very life."

Her grief and revelation came at him like a punch to his throat. He stepped back, his thoughts an incoherent, terrified jumble. "You saw Meera at the rehearsal."

She nodded, her chest heaving out a shuddering breath, but not crying. "I did. That mark she has through her left eyebrow… I'd know her in my sleep. I held her for a while before they took her away."

Simon took another step back, feeling as if the ground was being ripped from under him. "Did you know who I was? Did you know she's my daughter?" he demanded in a cold voice that was so unlike him that he hated it.

Her flinch told him how outlandish his accusation was. How much of a lie it made of everything they had shared. A desperate curse flew from his mouth and he thrust a hand through his hair. "Sorry." He kicked a pillar like a youth trying to work his temper out. "God, I'm so sorry. Of course you didn't know. That's why you looked as if you'd been kicked in the gut when we walked in together earlier."

Damn it, he should've never returned here with Meera. Never taken the chance on someone knowing her. But Rani had been the one who'd arranged everything with the adoption and he hadn't minded as long as she was happy. As long as they had a child to love.

A teen pregnancy, that's all they'd been told. A teen… He turned around, seeing the woman he'd thought so fragile, anew. "You…you had to have been so young."

"I was barely eighteen when I gave birth."

It hit him square in his gut. God, she'd been just a few years older than Meera now when she'd gotten pregnant, no more than a girl herself. He couldn't even imagine what it would have been like to be pregnant at that age. The man who was responsible… Every protective instinct in him roared at the very thought of a man who'd take advantage of a teenager.

"What happened to the man who fathered Meera?"

"He was a fortune hunter out for what he could get. He was nine years older than me, and he lavished me with attention I was desperate for. You see, I'd always had anxiety—even as a child—and it grew worse in my teens. The public nature of my parents' marriage, the constant media attention, the articles and interviews wondering if I was the talentless hack of the family…it made me such a ripe target for him. All he had to do was whisper a few empty promises and I gave myself over."

"He was a predator then. And no one can blame you for his actions. Not even yourself."

Something flickered in her eyes, making Simon want to pull her into his arms. Hold her again. Instead, he waited in silence, knowing she wanted to say more, holding the space for what had to be painful recollection.

"By the time I was ready to give birth, my mental health was at its worst. Not to mention I was anemic and far too thin. I couldn't trust my parents to keep my stuffed teddy bear safe let alone a baby," she said with no rancor, "Vikram was working night and day trying to dig us out of a financial pit and keep Virat from spiraling out of control, and my grandmother…she had her hands full keeping me alive and sane. I… I fought it so much back then but I'd have harmed Meera more if I'd kept her. I wasn't fit to be a parent."

"You don't owe me or anyone else an explanation,

Anya. Not for taking such a hard decision at such a young age."

"I want you to know that I gave her up because I wanted a better life for her," she said, her expression painfully earnest. "Not because I didn't love her."

Simon nodded, swallowing the ache her confession had lodged in his own throat. But whatever she'd gone through—however terrible it had been, it was in the past. As clinical and awful as it sounded in his mind, it wasn't his problem. Anya…and her grief weren't his to handle. Not that he'd proved himself any good at that when it had come to his wife.

He was only responsible for Meera and her well-being, thank God. Not this fierce but fragile woman.

"That choice meant she became our daughter, mine and Rani's," he said, without tempering the possessive claim in his voice. Without looking at the woman who seemed to wear her heart in her eyes. And in doing so weakened his resolve. "Rani adored Meera and gave up so much for her. Meera's her daughter, even more so than mine, I think."

"Of course she is," came Anya's voice, resolute and composed. "I didn't question that, not for a second."

Simon jerked his head around. But there was only calm acceptance in her eyes. Something about it steadied his own racing heartbeat.

He studied her—the composure she'd gained, the calm demeanor—and marveled at the strength of her. And yet, her grief was like a crackle of charge in the air, a shield she used to keep everyone out. He knew, without doubt, that she hadn't shared the news of her discovery with another soul. Not her brothers, not her sisters-in-law, not a friend.

And yet she'd told him.

Perversely, the trust she'd showed in him made his voice sharp as he said, "What do you want from me, Ms. Raawal?"

If she was hurt by how formal and terse he suddenly sounded, she didn't show it. He was beginning to realize that he had been a temporary escape for her, yes. But nothing more. Her attraction to him and everything that had followed between them meant very little in the bigger scheme of things like discovering the baby she'd given up.

As it should be.

"Nothing. I want nothing. Meera's adorable and funny and talented and well-adjusted and happy and above all, she's your daughter. I would never do anything to jeopardize her happiness, her sense of security. Ever."

He nodded, amazed by the strength of her will, by the grace with which she'd pulled herself together. "But? Because I'm sensing one," he said, a thread of anger in his tone.

But it was at himself, not her.

Was he already infatuated with this woman? Was it because he'd had sex with her, broken his years of celibacy with her that he was so tuned into her? Was it that for the first time in years his emotions were so sensitive to a particular woman's? Was it because she'd made him feel alive like no one else had in such a very long time?

Rani had always teased him that he was oblivious to all the emotional undercurrents in a room, that it took an elephant stomping around for him to realize that something was wrong. And yet, with this woman, he sensed and understood every nuance of emotion, every rise and dip of her mood. Worse, he was left only to admire her.

"I didn't plan for any of this," she said, a hint of steel creeping into her own tone now. "I didn't sit down and think… Gee, what am I going to do if I run into the precious baby I gave up thirteen years ago? Will I just idly stand by and watch her walk around without knowing who I am to her? Or hmm…will I mess everything up further by having wild, against-the-wall sex with her hot silver fox dad? Hmm…let's go with the second option because my life isn't exciting enough." Her chest was rising and falling by the time she finished her tirade, her beautiful brown eyes blazing with temper.

Simon laughed. So loudly that a couple of birds resting on the sill flew away.

She stared, stunned.

"Hot silver fox dad?" He'd never been able to flirt in his entire life and yet, that's what came out.

Her cheeks pink, Anya scowled at him. "I'm glad one of us finds this funny," she said with a sudden primness that he wanted to unravel all over again. Then she sighed. "You have to believe me that I didn't…"

"Don't, Anya," he said, her name falling off his lips so easily. Just once more, he promised himself, liking the taste of it on his tongue. "You don't have to apologize. Not to me or anyone." He thrust a hand through his hair, still feeling out of balance. "Neither do I forget for a single second how hard this must be for you. But damn it…"

"Can I ask you for just…one thing?" she said softly.

Simon nodded, knowing that he would agree to the most outrageous demand of hers if she looked at him like that with those big brown eyes and that ridiculously wide mouth and that earnest and somehow fierce expression.

"Please…don't change your plans because of me. Don't take her away from here because I'm here too. Don't let what happened between us…change your mind. All I want is to—" she looked up, as if the sky held all the answers "—to just see her for the few months of the shoot. I… I'd be content to just see her around the production schedule. I'm already…" Her throat bobbed up and down as she swallowed. "I'm so relieved and happy that she's been so well loved. I couldn't have asked for a better home for her. It's the one thing that makes all of the pain worth it."

"Meera's well-being matters more than anything to me." It was a reminder to him as much as it was for her. "I wasn't happy with her being here in the first place," he said, even though he hadn't decided to confide in her. "I… I don't like how this industry will prey on someone weak or young or innocent given a single chance."

"I'll keep an eye on her," she said, color blooming in her wan cheeks. "Without betraying who I am to her, I promise. My brother's production team is the safest place for her and I'm already on-site for the next few months as the costume designer. No one will question my presence around her. If it helps, you can even tell... Meera that you've asked me to keep an eye on her. That way, we're not deceiving her about my interest in her."

"Isn't that an added burden for you?"

She shook her head. "I'd have offered to do that for any young girl that came into the industry if I could. I was taken advantage of in my teens, remember. And that was despite my keeping a mostly low profile. Vikram regrets it to this day that he wasn't able to protect me better. Standing on the other side today, I can understand his pain after all these years."

Look at the two of them, being all adult and responsible and polite about this...

Simon wanted to believe it could stay mess free like this. That it wouldn't get all tangled in emotions. That this damned attraction between them, the intimacy they'd already shared wouldn't muck up everything again.

He gave her a nod and turned to go. Almost at the door that opened into the stairway, he said, "Why did you tell me?"

"What do you mean?"

"One would think I'm the last person you'd tell that you're the biological mother of my child. So why did you do it then?"

"I told you, I didn't plan for any of this."

As she walked toward him, Simon couldn't help but note the grace with which she moved, the core of steel beneath those tears and that panic. Beneath the fragile air that surrounded her, there was so much more to this woman. And that strength teased and tugged at him.

"Why shouldn't I tell you? This is your daughter I'm talking about. After that night, I feel as if…"

"It was just sex, Ms. Raawal," he said, infusing every ounce of remoteness he could manage into his words. "Damned good sex but that's all it was."

She tilted her chin. "I know that. But you were kind to me. That means whether you like it or not, I trust you. And I'd never do anything to hurt Meera. Or you."

That she added him in that vow made a pulse of emotions spear through him. When he just stared at her, she snapped, "Is there a reason you came after me tonight? The stranger you took against a wall in the darkness?"

Satisfaction glinted in her eyes at his continued silence. Their non-answer hung between them, more powerful than any words could conjure. "Maybe that's the very reason I couldn't keep it a secret from you. It felt like…playing games. I hate playing games with anyone's feelings. Especially when the stakes are this high." She rubbed a hand over her face, her jaw tight. "And God, I'm so tired of fate screwing me over. Again and again. This time, I'm going to drive this, not chance, not fate, not the past."

She walked past him, her head held high, leaving the scent of her skin lodged in his nostrils, and in his very lungs. And as much as he wanted to deny it, Simon knew he would never be able to think of her simply as the woman he'd had sex with in one moment of madness. Nor simply as the woman who'd given birth to Meera.

She was so much more than the sum of those things.

But he admired her too much already. For any of this to remain as uncomplicated as they both wished, he had no choice but to stay away from the woman. As much as was humanly possible.

CHAPTER FOUR

"You don't like my dad, do you?" asked Meera softly, panting while she walked fast on the treadmill.

The nib of Anya's pencil broke with a sharp click at Meera's sudden question. Anya took her time putting the pencil down and closing her sketchbook before she looked up at the chatty teenager.

Simon's matter-of-fact instructions to Meera that Anya was her unofficial companion when he wasn't around had been met with delight by the teenager. For some reason Anya didn't understand and could only marvel at, Meera considered Anya cool. In the last few days, Meera had thrown innumerable questions at Anya—about the Raawals, their stature in the industry, Anya's connections, her friends, her hobbies and which Bollywood star she currently had a crush on.

Anya had started showing up at the luxury hotel every morning, content to work on her sketches and designs while Meera finished her lessons in swordplay, archery and then wrapped up the rehearsals. If Virat thought it strange that Anya, who usually always preferred to work by herself until her sketches were ready for his input, was showing up at the preproduction every day, he didn't ask her any questions.

Despite her resolution that she'd see this time with her daughter as a gift and not get too attached, Anya knew she was more than halfway in love with the girl. There was something incredibly brave about Meera, much like the warrior queen she was playing in the movie. She seemed to breeze through life, informed about most things and intent on learning the rest.

Every day when their work ended, they'd eat while discussing any suggestions Meera had received from Virat, then she'd work out for about an hour. While her brother hadn't asked that Meera lose weight—Anya and Zara and Naina would have slaughtered him if he'd dared—he did want her to tone up to make the athletic swordplay and the fight scenes as authentic as possible.

If Meera's unending enthusiasm occupied Anya's day, thoughts about her dad consumed Anya's nights. If Simon's studious avoidance of her was anything to go by, he had no such problems.

"If it takes you this long to answer me, maybe I'm wrong and you do like him," Meera said, pulling Anya back to the present. Her hair pulled away from her plump face, the dim light in the gym casting half of it in shadows, she looked so much like Anya's mother, Bollywood's yesteryear superstar Vandana Raawal, that her breath caught in her throat.

"I don't know him well enough to like him or not like him," Anya said, courting diplomacy.

"It's just that," Meera said, huffing, "I've noticed that you…get very tense every time he comes around to pick me up. And Dad hasn't been himself lately so if he's said anything to upset you—"

A fierce heat claimed her cheeks. "Your dad and I hardly talk for him to offend me in any way."

"He doesn't like me being here—you know…getting into acting, I mean," Meera continued, thankfully ignorant of Anya's blush. "So if he did say anything to you about the Raawal House of Cinema or the movie industry, please don't take it personally." Meera wiped her face. "I don't want to lose you as a friend, Ms. Raawal. And not just because you're going to make me look like an amazing warrior queen. I just… I really like you."

Anya's chest tightened. "Of course you won't lose me. I'll be your friend for as long as you want," she added. "Nothing your dad says or does would change that, Meera."

There were so many questions she wanted to ask Meera but Anya rationed herself every day. Because she knew the risk of investing more and more of herself into this relationship. She knew that Meera would inevitably move on once this film was over, and when she did, she'd walk away with another piece of Anya's heart.

Despite the silent warning to herself, she couldn't stop asking, "What made you so interested in acting? Your…mother?"

She wasn't using the girl to satisfy her curiosity about the woman who'd owned Simon's heart. She wasn't.

There was an ache in her wide eyes as Meera thought of her mother, but there was also joy there too.

"Partly, yes. You know she retired before I was born. So I wasn't really immersed in that world growing up. But I loved watching her movies. Dad and I would pick one every Friday. She knew so much about so many people in the industry. She always indulged me when I asked for all the behind-the-scenes details and gossip." Meera hit Stop on the treadmill and grabbed a towel. "But at school, I seemed to naturally gravitate toward drama and dance. I just love everything about acting, you know? I mean, I'm adopted, so it can't be in the blood, but it definitely comes from somewhere."

Anya gasped. "What?"

"Oh, yeah, I'm adopted," Meera said, without even an ounce of anxiety in her tone. "Mama and Dad told me when I was seven. It didn't really make much of a difference to me. They *are* my parents."

Anya nodded, swallowing the knot in her throat. If she needed any proof that she'd done the right thing thirteen years ago, here it was. Her daughter was strong and well-adjusted, even with the loss she'd suffered at such a young age.

"I can imagine what your mother must have been like to have raised you to be such a wonderful girl," Anya whispered softly. From everything she was learning from Simon and Meera, Rani sounded like she'd been a wonderful woman. No wonder there had been such pain in Simon's expression every time he mentioned her.

Meera smiled. "I like to think she'd be proud of me. But I worry about Dad. He didn't really want to move back to Mumbai. I twisted his arm. But I did it as much for him as for me."

Anya knew she should stop this line of discussion immediately. Especially since just the mention of Simon's name had her pulse racing. She wanted to know nothing more about the man who already occupied too much of her thoughts and emotions. The man who'd brought her out of her shell.

The man who'd made her want so much out of life all of a sudden.

But when she looked at Meera, it was clear that the girl was desperate to share her worries with someone. "Why do you say that?" she prompted softly.

"He's been so lonely since Mama died. I know it's only been eighteen months, but I've never seen him so…withdrawn and grumpy as he's been recently. I struggled a lot in the beginning too. But he was wonderful to me. He didn't even get angry with me when he learned my grades were slipping. I feel as if he's still stuck there emotionally. I knew we had to get out of that empty flat and make a fresh start. So I made a huge ruckus after we met Virat sir at the mall. I whined constantly that Mama would never have said no to me, never would've stopped me trying…and that's when he finally agreed." A sheepishness filled Meera's face. "I kinda manipulated him. But I don't feel too bad about it, you know? I did it for his own good."

Anya laughed at the girl's innate confidence. "How is bringing your dad here for his own good?"

"Well, for one thing, he has some distant cousins

here. More importantly, his business partner and closest friend lives here. Ms. Sampson has visited us a few times after Mama died. I mean, she's definitely not who I want for a stepmother but…"

"Stepmother?" Anya said, aghast. "Your dad's marrying again?" The question burst out of her before she could judge the wisdom of asking the teenager about her dad's love life. Her heart was racing, her thoughts already spiraling into a loop.

Had Simon been in a relationship when he and Anya had…had sex that first night? Was he with her, even now, while Anya was obsessing over him? God, why was she obsessing over him?

It had been a moment of madness—utterly pleasurable madness, but still. Knowing now who he was to Meera, she could never indulge with him like that again. Not when she was finally albeit slowly coming out of her shell after all these years.

"I don't know," Meera said, tugging her hair back. "When we went to dinner on our second day back here, she was hinting pretty hard about how well-suited they are. And to be honest, whenever he sees her, Dad does cheer up a bit. I mean, it's not how Virat sir looks at Zara di or Vikram sir at Naina di," she added with a dreamy sigh and Anya giggled.

Her powerful brothers—known to be ruthless and caustic and brilliant—turned into completely different people around their wives. Their marriages had truly taken on a dreamy Bollywood-esque fairy-tale quality in the media for how real and passionate they were.

Something Anya couldn't even imagine for herself. That kind of love needed utter surrender and vulnerability and a kind of bravery she'd never had.

"But his marrying Ms. Sampson has to be better than him being lonely, right?" Meera asked morosely.

"You don't like her?" Anya said, frowning. Maybe she had no right to be jealous over some faceless woman, but she had every right to worry whether this woman would be kind to Meera as a stepmother.

"Not at all," Meera said without hesitation. "For one thing, she treats me like I was…six instead of thirteen. And she pretends all this interest in me in front of Dad but I can totally see through her. Pfft…she's not that good of an actress. She forgets I have Mama and Zara di for reference."

Anya couldn't help smiling at the girl's phrasing and took her hand. "Meera, it's not your job to worry over—"

"What's happened? Meera, what are you worrying about?" came Simon's deep voice behind them.

Releasing Meera's hand, Anya turned. Dressed casually in a light blue V-necked sweater and dark denim, Simon instantly dominated the vast gym area, his rugged masculinity in contrast with the overtly muscular look that was all the rage on cinema screens right now. The gray at his temples, the laughter lines around his mouth, the easy confidence with which he greeted everyone—from her brothers to the errand boy on set—made him the most potently real man Anya had ever met.

Meera scrunched her nose when Simon bent his head. "I'm all sweaty, Dad."

Simon kissed her cheek anyway. He cast Anya a quick but such a thorough glance that it sent a shiver down her spine before asking again, "What's got you worried, Meera?"

"Oh, just Virat sir's feedback today," Meera said without blinking. "If anyone can get me to quit acting, it's got be him."

"What?" They both responded though Simon's question came out in a thunderous growl. "Do you want me to talk to him?" Anya said, turning to her.

"God, no, I was just joking," Meera said, making a face. "Stop looking like that. Both of you. Everyone in the industry knows he's incredibly forthright when it comes to work. I've just got to grow a thicker skin." She turned to her dad. "I'm going to grab a quick shower." Meera looped her arm through Anya's, innocently fluttering her lashes at them. "Maybe Anya can join us for dinner?"

"No."

They both responded at the same time and with such emphasis that Meera's eyes went wide. "You know I thought I was imagining it, but I'm not. Why do you guys dislike each other?" she said, her tone suddenly petulant enough to remind Anya that she was a teenager who always wanted to have her own way.

"I don't dislike Ms. Raawal," Simon protested, his gaze holding Anya's. While every inch of his posture backed up his words, his eyes…his eyes said something else altogether. But Anya lacked both the confidence and the courage to call him on it.

"I've got to finish those initial sketches tonight," she mumbled, patting Meera's arm. "You just reminded me how Virat gets when he's in the thick of a project."

Hands on her hips, Meera turned her stubborn gaze to her dad, demanding an answer.

Simon sighed. "I haven't seen you much this week, Meera. I'd rather it just be the two of us this evening."

A whisper of dejection pinched Anya but she pushed it away. With Simon, she could always at least count on honesty. Grabbing her gym bag, Meera walked toward the bathroom.

Simon instantly switched his cell phone on, not even a little bothered by the cloud of awkwardness and tension swirling around them.

Anya stepped closer to him. The scent of him instantly made her belly tighten with longing. Both physical and…otherwise. Holding her spine straight took a lot of effort when all she wanted to do was to melt into his broad strength. "I need to talk to you."

Simon sighed, switched off his phone and tucked his hands into the pockets of his trousers. His whole "I'm bored with this conversation already" attitude made anger pour through Anya. "Yes, Ms. Raawal. What is it?"

"Don't 'Ms. Raawal' me as if I'm another teenager bothering you."

She sighed, instantly regretting her curt tone. He wasn't acting any differently from what they'd agreed to be going forward—polite strangers.

But this suave, remote Simon…made her feel so unsure of herself. "That night…when we…"

He raised a brow, an unholy light suddenly shimmering in his eyes. "When we…what?" he teased.

"When you and I…" Anya said, licking her dry lips and casting a quick glance in the direction that Meera had gone in, "when we had—" she lowered her voice to a bare whisper, but it took another swallow to get the word out "—*sex*, were you…already in a relationship with someone else?"

The thread of humor in his beautiful eyes disappeared. His thick brows knotted into a scowl and the step he took toward Anya had her backing up against the wall.

He swore. "Stop acting as if you're scared of me."

"Of course I'm not," she retorted, feeling hot all over.

"Is that why you scurried off and hid in the bathroom for five minutes last time I picked up Meera?"

So he had noticed that. "I'm just…" She rubbed a hand over the nape of her neck. "Being near you does a number on me, okay?"

That answer burned away the quick flare of his temper. But a shimmer of a remote coolness remained. "Are you asking me if I was cheating on someone with you, Angel?"

His frigid tone was answer enough and still, some wild, wanton part of Anya didn't want to release him yet. Because she had a strange feeling that she had a hold on him just then. He didn't like that she could think him capable of something like that. "It's just…"

She swallowed Meera's name, feeling heat creep up her cheeks. "Something made me wonder."

When the glacial coolness in his eyes didn't thaw, Anya pushed at his chest with her palms, a strange belligerence rising up in her. "It's not my fault if I did wonder, is it? We barely knew each other and ever since…you've been acting as if I'll proposition you if you so much as look at me. I thought with everything that happened, we were friends at least."

"You're even more naive than I assumed if you think we could be friends after what's happened." His voice softened, as if he was trying to not upset her delicate sensibilities. That in turn only angered her.

"So you weren't cheating then? You weren't with anyone else romantically?" she probed shamelessly, wanting to know if he was in a relationship with Ms. Sampson now.

"No, I wasn't. Even when Rani and I were married…" He exhaled roughly, biting away the rest. "And that ends this discussion."

Anya's curiosity about his marriage, about his loyalty to his wife, about everything related to him, basically, went up another notch. "I'm sorry if I implied you were capable of infidelity."

"You're forgiven," he said with an ease that said he'd grant her anything if she just stopped talking to him.

"But I do have something else important I want to talk to you about. Why don't we meet during lunch tomorrow here at the hotel? Meera and my brothers will be busy. My suite is out of everyone's way and we can—"

"Are you asking me over for an afternoon quickie, Angel?"

"What?" Her pulse raced at the very idea, her body softening at the picture her overimaginative brain painted immediately. Quickie or not, this time she'd make sure there was a bed available. Definitely.

Simon tapped her shoulder, grinning wickedly. "I was just kidding."

"I know that. And of course I'm not inviting you for a—" she lowered her voice again "—quickie."

He shrugged. "I can't have lunch with you tomorrow. I'm…busy."

"Simon, this is—"

"Good evening, Ms. Raawal," he pronounced stiffly in a raised voice.

Anya looked behind her to see Meera had just emerged from the bathroom at the other end of the long gym. She pressed a hand to Simon's chest and leaned closer. He straightened from his relaxed stance, tension swathing him at her touch. She bent and whispered, "So you're available for the quickie but not to talk?"

Without waiting for his answer, Anya pulled away, a feral satisfaction flooding her at his stunned gaze. Pasting a beaming smile to her lips, she bid Meera a quiet good-night and walked away on trembling knees.

Before the infuriating man tempted her to more unwise actions.

She was playing with fire—and thank God he hadn't called her bluff. No way could she do the casual thing with him again. But she also didn't remember a moment where she'd felt so alive in her entire life.

* * *

Long after Meera went to bed, Simon poured himself a drink at the bar and wandered toward the terrace attached to the penthouse. The night was balmy and muggy with a storm in the making.

Despite the fact that the penthouse at the hotel—one of his own group—was the height of luxury, he didn't like the temporariness of it any more than he'd liked the empty silence of their home in Singapore over the last year and a half. It smacked of uncertainty. After growing up with a single parent who'd dragged him up and down the country in search of work, Simon didn't like not having a solid home base. They could choose any one of his residences in a number of the big cities in India, but this was where Meera wanted to be now.

Where she was thriving.

Yet the fact that Meera was thriving in an over-whelmingly demanding industry, in a new city, amid strangers, was, he knew, in no small way thanks to Anya's calming, serene influence. Not even ten days had passed since they'd met and already he could see her stable hand guiding Meera's impulsive nature to make better choices.

And just like that, the real source of his unease be-came crystal clear. It had less to do with the fact that his life and Meera's were in a flux right now and more to do with the woman who'd just walked into their lives like Mumbai's monsoon season.

Even the smallest interaction with her began a clam-oring in his gut for more…

His muscles tightened at the memory of Anya's palm

pressed against his abdomen not a few hours ago. The subtle jasmine scent of her as she'd bent her head and taunted him. The tease of her hair against his jaw, the naked desire she'd let him see in her eyes for a split second…

So you're available for the quickie but not to talk…

The raw, wanton pleasure they'd shared that first evening together was never far from his mind. But when Anya stood close to him like that… Simon wanted far too much. Not just of her, but of himself, of his life. Desires and dreams he'd written off long ago reared up again now, slithering hungrily through him.

If he hadn't spied Meera emerging from the bathroom, he didn't know what he'd have done at Anya's husky challenge.

No, who was he kidding?

He knew exactly what he'd have done.

He'd have pressed the saucy minx against the wall and captured those pretty lips with his. He'd have kissed the hell out of her right there, uncaring of who might walk in—her brothers, Meera, the entire damned world for all he cared. He'd have dragged her up to another one of those shadowy corners and proceeded with the quickie that they both so badly wanted. Then he'd have taken her to her bedroom and spent the whole night proving to her that this fire between them wouldn't die with one orgasm or ten.

Clutching the metal sill of the balcony tight until his knuckles turned white, Simon willed his rising libido to calm down. There was no release for him coming anytime soon. Especially not with the one woman he wanted.

And he couldn't even blame her because he was the one who'd brought up the idea of another round of sex in the first place. He'd wanted to shake her up. Wanted to have a little petty revenge at the fact that she'd dare think so little of him that he'd be unfaithful to anyone he cared for. So he'd tugged the one thread that seemed to bind them together. Just her and him. Selfishly, he'd wanted it to be the thread that had nothing to do with Meera or how desperately Anya wanted to be a part of his daughter's life.

The look in her eyes when she'd asked if he'd made her a party to cheating, the way it took her so long to say the word *sex*…it was a good reminder that Anya Raawal was the last woman he could have a temporary, secret affair with.

And that's all he could offer her. Not counting the fact that between her brothers and his daughter, it wouldn't remain a secret for too long.

She wanted to be part of Meera's life, not his. She was far too young for him, and by her own admission, she'd barely dipped her toe into romantic relationships. "Made for love and marriage" might as well have been stamped on her forehead for how generous hearted she was, how achingly lovely she was.

Eventually, she'd want things he didn't want to give, couldn't give another woman. Like marriage and children and…love. Eventually, she'd look at him as Rani had looked at him at the end—with resentment and anger and bitterness. It had eaten away at them both like acid, killing any love they'd once felt for one another.

Even the thought of that bitterness in Anya's eyes, hurt pinching that lush mouth…was unbearable.

He couldn't afford for history to repeat itself. And this time with a woman who was even more fragile and innocent than Rani had ever been.

CHAPTER FIVE

ANYA STUDIED THE carefully curated pictures on Leila Sampson's social media feed, anxiety and something else rising up within her belly like an impending storm. In the last month, every fourth picture that had been posted was of her and Simon. In a variety of his hotel locations, the latest in Thailand and Seychelles.

While none of them were intimate poses—and a dark emotion that tasted very like jealousy gripped Any at the thought—it was clear that, whatever the nature of their relationship, Simon was spending every spare moment with the other woman.

The last few weeks had been bad enough in terms of how distracted she'd been at work. Predictably, Virat had torn her initial sketches into shreds—literally and figuratively. For the first time in her life, Anya wasn't able to give her all to her work.

If it was only because she was spending more time with Meera, Anya could have made her peace with it. But she couldn't ignore the fact that a large part of her brain was occupied with Simon and what was becoming increasingly obvious—whatever he'd claimed before, the man was now getting serious about Leila Sampson.

And ever since Leila had been caught coming out of a couture wedding gown designer's studio after a personal consultation, Anya had had trouble sleeping. The gossip was all over social media.

Millionaire widower looking for love again?

Once the big love of our beloved star actress Rani Verma's life, real estate magnate Simon De Acosta's back in Mumbai to keep a close eye on his daughter Meera Verma's acting debut with the prestigious Raawal House of Cinema!

As if that wasn't exciting enough for us, Simon has a new lady love. When questioned about their plans, real estate heiress Ms. Leila Sampson revealed exclusively to us that things are moving fast between her and Simon. But what kind of woman would have the guts to fill the shoes of the brilliant, beautiful and beloved Rani Verma?

Despite all the stern lectures she'd given herself to stay out of Simon's private life, Anya had to do something. The man had left her no choice at all.

If he was determined to marry a woman without considering Meera's future happiness, then Anya would remind him that he'd gotten his priorities all wrong. And for Meera, who'd innocently told Anya where Simon would be, she would even venture out of her shell and accost the man at one of those parties that she usually avoided like the plague.

Desperate times called for desperate measures.

The party hadn't been as boring and nerve-racking as Anya had assumed it would feel. She'd run into a couple of familiar faces and found it easy, even effortless to catch up. People who'd asked after her latest designs, about when she was traveling again…friends she'd kept at a distance because she'd thought all their interest in her was only because she was a Raawal.

Of course, there were opportunists and social climbers and even predators in the industry, but how had she become so distrustful of everyone? So afraid of her own shadow? Why had it taken her this long to step back into her own life and look outside of its margins?

She didn't know if it was because she'd discovered Meera, or because of the bold step she'd already taken with Simon, but Anya felt this new…fizz of excitement in her belly for all the possibilities that were suddenly open to her.

But not for a second did she forget why she was at the party. All evening, she'd kept an eye on Simon and Leila, the possessive way the latter had clung to Simon. There was a familiarity in how they talked to each other but not once did Anya see him give the other woman his undivided attention. He also never touched her like he had Anya. So why was he marrying her then?

As the party wound down and guests began to drift into smaller groups, Anya, like an unscrupulous PI or journalist shamelessly followed the couple into the beautiful gazebo set in the expansive lawn. String lights and paper lanterns hung from trees, making the garden a perfect destination for lovers. And yet the argument that Anya had sensed brewing between the couple all evening finally seemed to blow up. The stiffness of Simon's gestures as he faced the other woman took away the last hesitation Anya felt in interrupting them like a crazy groupie.

Neither did she miss the irony in the fact that she was judging Leila for clearly marking her territory when it came to Simon when Anya herself was this close to stalking the man. Of course, her primary motivation was Meera's well-being, she convinced herself. Though she was beginning to wonder if there was a lot more to it than that.

Refusing to back out now, Anya moved toward him. "Simon…" She forced out a laugh which sounded utterly fake to her own ears. "It is you."

His head jerked in her direction, searching for her in the darkness. The planets had to be on her side because Leila Sampson's cell phone trilled at that moment. With one glance at her phone, then at Simon, she left.

Heart racing, Anya felt his gaze move over her face, then do a quick once-over of her body as if he was tracing the contours with those rough fingers. That single glance was enough to start a powerful hum beneath her skin.

She watched greedily as his long, powerful strides covered the distance between them, moonlight gilding the breadth of his shoulders, the tapering of his hips, the muscled thighs. Revealing him bit by bit, unwrapping him bit by bit, for her very own pleasure. Around him, Anya felt like a feral, possessive creature. A feeling she didn't want to trust but couldn't ignore either.

Hopefully hiding the intensity of her awareness, she beamed at him. Because she knew, on an instinctive level, that Simon should never know how much she longed to kiss him again. How much she thought of him, how much she liked herself when she was with him.

"Ms. Raawal," he said, a hint of humor pulsing beneath the stiff formality of his address. His white linen shirt lovingly molded to the broad span of his chest and there was so much of him she longed to reach out and touch.

Her fingers twitching, Anya cursed herself for the non-intimacy of their one-night stand. She'd gotten no chance to explore his gorgeous body at all. "Fancy seeing you here tonight."

"I should be the one surprised," he said, his eyes gleaming. "Meera informs me—frequently and volubly—that you strictly avoid this kind of gathering."

"Meera's right. But I've long been a fan of Ustadji's music so I made an exception tonight."

"I noticed how lost you were to the music," he said, surprising her. She hadn't known he was aware of her presence even. He rubbed a finger over his brow and almost glared at her. "It seems you draw people to you as effortlessly as the rest of your family." The humor lingered in his tone but there was something sharp in that statement that reminded her of the man who'd granted her everything she'd once asked for under the cover of darkness.

That small shift in his tone made liquid warmth unspool in her lower belly. At the simple knowledge that he'd been as aware of her throughout the evening as she'd been of him. "If you're talking about Ustadji's son asking for my phone number," she said, heat rising in her cheeks, "that man is an irresistible poet in addition to the soulful music he produces. Magic in his fingers and words."

"And?"

Anya pulled the edge of her shawl tighter as it slid from her shoulders. "And what?" she said, sensing the energy between them shift and grow. Becoming more than that constant hum.

"Are you going to take him up on his offer?"

Anya so desperately wanted to flutter her eyelashes and play coy. But it was more than her aversion for the limelight that had kept her from acting. She was bad at dissembling. Bad at playing games and pretending. Bad at acting as if she could just forget that night with him had happened.

"I enjoyed tonight more than I'd expected. But I'm not sure about…seeing him again."

"Good."

The emphasis in his word reverberated in the air between them. It felt like he was throwing a gauntlet down and it set her teeth on edge. Her spine stiffened and she realized maybe it wasn't a bad thing to be like her brothers. They were arrogant and determined but they were also brave and loyal and hid hearts of gold.

And it had taken them every single ounce of that courage to win their wives.

While Anya wasn't looking for love, this thing with Simon…this relationship they were having without calling it so, needed all her wits. Maybe she needed to own up to having a little Raawal blood in her. Maybe it wasn't all a bad thing after all.

"I might change my mind though," Anya added, her voice low. "I know I should stop hiding so much, live life a little more. The last time I did that, I found it extremely…*rewarding*."

He stepped toward her, sucking out all the oxygen from around them. At least that's how it felt to her lungs. "Do you plan to go out and have a *rewarding* experience every time the fancy strikes you?"

"Maybe. No, the answer is yes. Definitely yes."

"Is that such a good idea, Ms. Raawal?"

Anya took another step, feeling as if she was sitting at the very top of a roller coaster. About to drop off the edge. She knew she was going to scream, she knew she was going to have the time of her life, but there was only a little fear. Mostly, there was this…violent excitement in her limbs, anticipation a ball in her chest.

She reached out and delicately flicked the edge of his collar, as if she was dusting off a leaf or a petal. Barely touching him but wanting to claim a small part of him. "Maybe you shouldn't be butting into my life while you call me Ms. Raawal in that forbidding tone?"

Tension rolled off him in waves. "I have no right to forbid you from doing anything. But as someone who's aware of the distressing discovery you made not that long ago, in fact as the only one who knows of it, I'm more than entitled to caution you."

"And what is the caution you think I should exercise?"

"You should be careful with whom you…associate, Angel. You're in a vulnerable place."

"Associate…hmm," Anya said softly, a thread of hurt winding itself around her heart. "So having sex with you is okay even though you were a stranger but it's wrong to do it with someone who's not you?"

His nostrils flared but his voice stayed low, steady. "That's not at all what I said. Even as an outsider to the industry, I know the kind of games Ustadji's son is known for. You were lucky with me. Not every stranger is going to be…"

"As generous and giving as you were?"

"As harmless as me." He pushed a hand through his hair, his frustration translating itself to Anya. He obviously didn't want any kind of relationship with her, but he didn't want her to be friendly with any other man? She shouldn't have been able to understand that but strangely, she did.

"You said Meera was your priority right now," he added.

"If you're worried that I might turn into some kind of bad influence on Meera, you should…"

His fingers landed on her chin, tilting her up to meet his eyes. Just the tips of two fingers and yet, she felt the contact all over her body. "I don't think that at all. I… I'm only thinking of you. Damn it, I feel responsible, Angel. For you."

Something about the possessive gleam in his eyes, the firm grip of his fingers, the scent of him filling her nostrils, her very lungs, goaded Anya. "What shall I do then, Simon? Lock myself away for another decade? Or should I just call you when I need a reward for good behavior?"

Simon pulled away his fingers, as if her words burned him. "Why are you really here tonight, Anya?"

"I've something important to say to you," she said, trying to find her way through the dark. They were moving farther away from the gazebo and the fairy lights.

"Talk then," he said, his hand immediately grasping her elbow when she stepped onto an uneven path.

A cold breeze flew past and Anya pulled the shawl around her neck tighter. Instantly, Simon pulled her against his body as if he meant to shield her from the elements. By the time they reached the outer edge of the gardens, hidden from the other guests, her resolve that she was only doing this for Meera's sake weakened.

Whatever he saw in her face, Simon's mouth tightened. "You're nervous."

Anya scrunched her nose. "A little."

"Did something happen with Meera?"

"No," she hurried to reassure him. "Well, there's the thing with one of the young light boys but I dealt with it."

He scowled. "What is the thing with the light boy?"

"A harmless crush."

"For God's sake, she's only thirteen. What did he do?"

"He? He did nothing. She's the one who keeps finding reasons to talk to him. If you didn't know this about her already, she's bold as brass."

Mouth pursed tight, Simon looked like he still wanted to find the light boy and straighten him out.

"Meera's fine," she repeated. "We all went to get ice cream together. I sat at a different table and they talked for a little bit. She has no friends of her own age here yet, Simon. This is good for her."

"You're not a parent. You don't know that."

Anya flinched. Just because she'd spent the better part of three weeks with Meera now, didn't mean Anya knew everything about parenting. But try as she might, his words hurt.

He raked a hand through his hair and grabbed her wrist gently. "I...didn't mean that the way it sounded."

"I know that," Anya said softly. Why the hell was it so easy to trust this man? Why him when he clearly didn't want to have anything to do with her? "It has come to my notice that you're getting serious about Ms. Sampson," she blurted out, reminding herself why she was here.

"And who brought you this notice?"

His dry tone made Anya flush, but she went on. "Apparently, she and you are planning to buy a villa together...and she's getting an exclusive designer wedding gown designed for her."

Simon's gaze turned inscrutable and Anya had no way of knowing if he knew of it already.

Had he already proposed? Had they even set a date?

Dark and bitter, jealousy twisted her gut as she considered the possibility that soon even thinking about

Simon when she went to bed alone, when she tried to imitate his caresses would be forbidden, since he'd belong to someone else. Even this easy camaraderie and strange intimacy they shared—despite his determination to keep her at a distance—she'd have no right to enjoy.

"And where did you see this?"

"On Ms. Sampson's social media."

His thick brows rose. "You've been spying on her?"

"I went straight to the source instead of listening to the media's speculations, that's all."

One corner of his mouth twitched and Anya had a feeling he was enjoying her discomfiture too much. But at least he wasn't angry, thank God.

"And now you've accosted me at a party to what? Congratulate me?"

"I thought someone should tell you that Meera doesn't like her at all. In the role of a stepmother, that is." When his silence began leaching away her courage, Anya just plowed on, her genuine concern for Meera overtaking her innate resistance to the rude way she was barging into his personal life. "And more importantly, she thinks Ms. Sampson neither likes her nor cares about her."

"And you're the expert on Ms. Sampson now?"

Anya didn't miss the fact that he hadn't denied her claim. "I simply choose to trust Meera's judgment. As you very well know, she's desperate for you to be happy. She even mentioned that if marrying Ms. Sampson is what it takes for you to be happy, she'll bear it. But I don't think that's fair at all. She's just thirteen, she lost her mother not eighteen months ago and she's handling a new career in another country. She shouldn't have to put up with a woman who only pretends an interest in her on top of everything else."

His fingers cupped her shoulder, his mouth flat. "Wait, go back. Meera wants me to be what?"

Anya sighed, relief crashing through her. It was clear that he had no idea of Meera's concerns for him. "Meera's worried about you. She talks of you and your loneliness and how…lost you've been the last year and a half. She totally adores you, Simon, and thinks Rani's death has…changed you in ways she doesn't understand."

His jaw tightened as he released her. His gaze cut away from her as if he didn't want to share even a bit of his grief with her. "I lost my wife in a car accident. It should change me."

Anya's chest tightened. But there was more than simple grief there. "I'm not questioning why she feels like that. And I didn't mean to pile on any guilt. I'm just…"

"Sharing one evening with me doesn't give you the right to interfere in my life."

His words, delivered in a cold, flat tone, landed hard. As he'd meant for them to. "But being someone who loves Meera unconditionally, someone who's desperately wishing for a chance to be part of her life permanently, I have the right to ask. I have the right to point out that you might be making a wrong decision," Anya rallied valiantly.

"Neither Meera nor you know what it's been like for

me." He glared at her, as if daring her to argue. "As for the matter of Leila, not that it's any of your—"

"If anyone should be Meera's mother, it should be me. And we both know that at least the sex between us would be fantastic!"

He rounded on her, his jaw slackened incredulously.

Anya clamped her hand over her mouth, her pulse racing madly all over. She hadn't realized what she meant to say until the words had just popped out. Until her brain grabbed them out of air and conjured the image of a future that teased Anya's imagination. She waited for a thread of fear to filter through. The thought of a future with a man—someone who could break her trust all over again, someone who would only see her for what he could get out of her—had always terrified her before. And yet nothing came when she thought of Simon and Meera in her life. Nothing but an unbidden, unwanted thrill shooting through her.

"Is that a proposal, Angel?"

Embarrassment made her skin heat. "It's not what I meant to say but it's better than you marrying a woman who barely tolerates Meera, isn't it?" Anya retorted, bristling. "No other woman in your life will love Meera more wholeheartedly than I already do. And if you're also getting married for regular sex—hello, ding-ding-ding…? We have a winner there too," she said, moving her hand between them. "I don't have much experience with men, as you know, but the kind of chemistry we have… I think it should work for even the irregular kind of sex too."

"What's irregular sex? How long have I been celibate for? Did they invent a new kind of sex while I was away from the dating scene?"

Her cheeks were on fire and he was laughing at her now but still, her determination and desperation wouldn't stop the words from bubbling over. "No, I mean just not traditional sex. But like fun sex. Not that what we did at the hotel was traditional… In fact, I think it kinda straddled the line between traditional and fun…"

"Thank the Lord! For a moment there I was afraid of what I'd missed!"

Anya swatted him. "You're making fun of me!"

His eyes were wide pools of laughter; his broad chest shook with it. He looked so breathtakingly gorgeous when he laughed like that she only half minded that she'd just made a complete fool of herself. "You're making it irresistible not to."

With a gasp of outrage, she turned and threw her hand out almost losing her balance. He caught it and tugged. The momentum made her stumble and he caught her too and before she knew it, Anya banged her hip into his front. His curse was loud and colorful in the quiet garden as her nose bumped against his jaw. Still he didn't let her go. "Are you hurt?"

The corded strength of him surrounded her, taking her breath away. "Only my ego," she said softly, pressing her hand to his jaw, wanting desperately to soothe him. Wanting to touch him all over. Just once, God, just once, she wanted her hands all over him—over every hard contour, every solid sinew, every tight muscle. She wanted to rake her nails over his broad pecs, test the give of his ridged abdomen with her teeth. She wanted to mark him all over until the thought of every other woman—the ghost of his ex, and his very current business partner—was driven from his mind.

The strength of her possessive instincts sent a flurry of alarm through her. And still, she couldn't pull away.

"Are you?" she asked, her thumb moving to the sharp jut of his prominent cheekbones and over the hollow underneath.

"Of course I'm not hurt." His fingers grabbed her wrist to stop the motion but stilled. "Except you are making me lose my mind."

She bit her lip, her fingers relishing the raspy sensation of his evening stubble. "I didn't mean for this—"

"Stop touching me," he muttered. Perversely, a second before his mouth covered hers.

His lips were hungry and desperate and hard but only for a few seconds. Wrapping her arms around his muscled back, Anya pressed herself into him in silent surrender. Instantly, his kiss softened, his caresses gentled, transformed into something else.

Tender and hot and…exploratory. He tasted her, tempted her, teased her without the urgency that had swamped them in the darkness at the hotel. Fingers buried in her hair, her body arched into him so that she could feel the imprint of his growing erection against her belly. He riled up her passion and soothed it all at the same time in a devilishly thorough kiss.

It was the first kiss they should've had if Anya's discovery about Meera hadn't plunged her into a kind of temporary madness. This was a "do you want to do this with me" kiss. His lips were soft and yet firm, pressing forward and then retreating, inviting her to play, inviting her tongue to dance with his. Inviting her to enjoy just this moment with him.

They kissed for what felt like an eternity to her, Simon pulling away just when Anya needed her breath and pressing her down onto a stone bench. And then coming back before she could recover her equilibrium. The lazy swirl of his tongue inside her mouth, the soothing strokes of his hands over her back, the way he peppered her jaw and neck with his kisses before finding his way back again to her sensitized lips, there was no destination, no rush to do anything except savor this moment. To just be.

Clinging to him like a jasmine creeper to the wall, Anya gave in to the delicious torment. And it was exactly what she'd needed from the moment she'd discovered he was Meera's adoptive father. From the moment he'd become forbidden to her. From the moment she'd realized they were now connected by something that neither of them had chosen, that whatever had happened between them already was the most they could ever have.

She'd needed to know that Simon still wanted her. After everything she'd revealed, after everything that had passed between them. And he did want her. This kiss told her that beyond a doubt.

The realization unraveled the tangle of her own emotions. She wondered if, in her heart of hearts, this was what she'd come here for tonight. If the ridiculous proposal of marriage that had fluttered onto her lips was her subconscious telling her she wanted far more of Simon in her life. That her interest in him had so much more to do with him as a man than simply the fact that he was Meera's father.

Not a month ago, she'd been content to hide, to live her life in the margins.

And now, now it seemed all she wanted to do was jump straight off the cliff.

Because there was no doubt, she reminded herself even as every inch of her body ached for his complete possession, that indulging in the idea of Simon as some kind of romantic partner—even a temporary one—was nothing short of jumping off a cliff to a very messy end.

Anya was the softest, sweetest thing he'd ever kissed. A shaft of moonlight crossed her face in a beam, highlighting the swollen plumpness of her lips. Even that wasn't enough of a reminder to stop Simon. One arm cupping the nape of her neck, he lapped at her lips until she gave in one more time. She sank into the kiss with a soft moan that reverberated through him, warming up every limb, waking up every dormant need.

Her fingers tugged at the lapels of his shirt, her mouth pulling back from his just enough for her to speak. "How can you kiss me like this and think of marrying another woman?" Vulnerability sparked in her question, in the soft, curious slant of her eyes.

With a pithy curse, Simon wrenched himself away from her. Pulling her knees up into her chest, Anya stayed on the stone bench, looking painfully innocent.

His body was shaking and incredibly aroused, his

breath coming in shallow spurts. "I'm sorry," he whispered. "For kissing you like that. For acting like a thorough hypocrite."

She gave him her sharp profile in reply.

He wished she would berate him for acting like a rogue. Worse, for blowing hot and cold on her. Instead, when she spoke again, her voice was a sweet whisper. "I like it when you kiss me. It makes me feel brave, different, wanted. As if—"

"It was a slip. And it doesn't change anything, Angel. You and I can have nothing more than Meera in common. And that's enough of a complication as it is."

He saw the movement of her Adam's apple, the thread of hurt she tried to hide. "You keep saying that. But it doesn't mean I can't enjoy it when I overwhelm your reason."

He smiled despite everything, the open admission sending warmth through his veins.

She straightened to her feet. The loose V-necked top she wore hung on her slender frame and yet, she looked so starkly sensual that Simon's pulse beat erratically. Dark skinny jeans molded to her long legs. The cashmere shawl hung at her elbows, a flimsy protection against the cool night. Her beautiful eyes glimmered in the faint moonlight, resolve etched into her stubborn features. "You never answered my question."

"For God's sake, I've no intention of ever marrying again. I've barely recovered from the last time."

She took a step back, her gaze wide and searching at his blunt admission. Could she see that what she thought was grief in his eyes was actually crippling guilt? "You are...not marrying Leila then?"

"No."

"Oh."

"Would you like to take back your oh-so-romantic proposal now?" he asked, enjoying her discomfiture far too much.

Her fingers tightened around the edges of her shawl. "Yes, I think so."

He pressed a palm to his chest, curving his mouth in a mocking laugh. "Wow, first the assumption that I'd marry anyone without first considering Meera's happiness. Then the withdrawal of your proposal. You came packed tonight, Angel."

"I'm sorry for assuming you wouldn't consider Meera, but everything pointed to..."

Simon thrust a hand roughly through his hair. "Look, Leila is my oldest friend and business partner. Which, believe me, has given me enough insight into her character. I'm aware that she has no interest whatsoever in Meera. And while I don't hold it against her, I'm also aware it would make her a very poor choice of wife for me. Despite what she thinks."

"So she does want to marry you?"

"I'm not answering that, Ms. Raawal."

"Ms. Raawal? Are we really back to that again? And why not answer me?"

"All you need to know is that no woman will try to push you out of Meera's life. No woman, other than her mother, has a claim on her affections. Now, I'd prefer it if could you untangle your emotions about me and

Meera in your head." He sent her a confused face a hard glance, carefully picking his words. "It would be nice if you stopped throwing yourself at me just to remain close to my daughter."

"That's an awful thing to say!" she gasped.

He remained silent, his blood pounding in his ears.

Outrage sparked in her eyes as she covered the distance between them. "If you must know," she said, poking him in his chest, her hair mussed from his fingers, her mouth swollen and pink, looking so delectable that it took all he had to not throw her over his shoulder and steal her away all over again, "what I want to do with you has nothing to do with Meera. It has nothing to do with logic or self-preservation or common sense. And it terrifies me to my soul.

"What I want with you is…simply you. I want you for you, Simon. For your kisses. For your kindness. For the generous, honorable man you are even when that results in you pushing me away. God help me, I don't know how to stop this wanting."

Before Simon could respond to that heated declaration, she stomped away from him, her back rigid, her steps sure.

For long minutes after she left, he stood there, his ruffled ego soothed by her passionate declaration, his body tight and hungry for release, his emotions in as big a tangle as their old string of Christmas lights in Meera's hands.

He'd had no problem rejecting Leila's suggestion that they wed earlier that evening, or holding out against her rational arguments when he'd refused. But deep down in his soul, Anya Raawal and her...horribly awkward but endearing non-proposal tempted him.

She tempted him. To no end.

No one made him laugh like she did.

No one made him come alive like she did.

No one made him want to abandon the little common sense he had left in him and simply seduce her, take whatever she was willing to give him.

For once, Simon wanted to be totally selfish and damn the consequences to hell. He wanted the joy and unfettered pleasure Anya Raawal brought to his life by her mere presence.

He wanted to be the Simon he'd glimpsed in her eyes.

CHAPTER SIX

THE LAST THING Anya had expected when she walked into the MahaRani suite at the beautifully renovated luxury hotel—historically called the Palace of Mirrors—in Udaipur for the shoot location was to find her brothers and Simon waiting on her.

It had been a surprise when the production coordinator had directed her to this hotel when her brothers and the crew were staying closer to the set a few kilometers away. Not that she had any complaints about a stay in the luxurious hotel—even Vikram with all his reach hadn't been able to book this suite last year when he'd wanted to impress Naina.

Until she had stepped into the beautiful foyer and realized the hotel and its recent renovation from a dilapidated palace was one of Simon's recent projects.

The suite she'd been accorded was vast, luxurious, with a private courtyard and a pool in the back. A gazebo, assumed to be the secret meeting place of two local lovers, sat on the edge of the beautiful pool like the pendant on a pearl necklace. As a history buff, there was nothing she liked more than to study local history, mine the rich folktales, try to see the past come alive through clothes and architecture and weaponry that had once been used.

With Simon standing on one side of the sitting lounge, both her brothers on the other, and Zara and Naina sitting on a luxurious settee in between them, it was as if one of the local battles was about to take place in this very suite. She didn't even have a moment to marvel at the thick Persian rug under her feet or the classy royal procession wallpaper design that gave the suite an utterly elegant, almost royal look.

Dumping her handbag and overnight bag on an armchair that had heavy dark wood and modern upholstery in a perfect marriage of old and new, she stole a surreptitious glance at Simon first.

Seeing him here in her suite, three days after she'd made that foolishly passionate declaration about how much she wanted him, after they'd shared such a raw, needy kiss was shock enough. But to face him with her brothers watching on… Anya rubbed a hand over her temple, more than physical exhaustion catching up with her.

With all the decisions she'd been making recently, she had known that some version of her brothers butting in would happen soon. But she'd naively hoped for it to be later rather than sooner.

She'd barely slept in the last three days. The costume designs she'd been working on for Zara and Meera had finally clicked. With Virat's demand for perfection in every small detail, they were nowhere near finalized. But he had said "brilliant" to her, and that was high praise indeed. After his approval, she'd gone into a frenzy with her production team to get them finished in time for the costume rehearsal. She'd been working long hours at her workshop, where she worked with some of the best seamstresses and tailors in the country.

It was a world of its own—her sanctuary when reality became too much for her. And maybe, just maybe, she'd also been hiding from her own desperate need to see Simon again.

Anya had no doubt that Naina's and Zara's presence was to corral her brothers' inclination to be overly protective of her. No one else dared to try, much less succeed.

"What? Is there something on my face?" she barked at her brothers, her crankiness coming out at impending family drama.

This was her fault. She'd let them cocoon her and cosset her for far too long. Now, they'd have trouble accepting that she could think and act for herself.

"Why didn't you tell us?" Vikram demanded.

Virat simply studied her.

"Tell you what?" Anya asked.

"Have you looked at any social media recently, Anya?" Zara asked in a soft, concerned tone.

Her heart thudded against her rib cage, fear snaking through her veins like tendrils taking root. "Not at all. I've been at the workshop. There's barely any internet connection there and I like it like that." Her hands shook as she unraveled the scarf from around her neck. God, what had they written about her family now?

"Is it about Mama and Papa?"

"No," Virat spoke finally. "It's about you."

About her? About her and who? What about her?

Her gaze instantly sought Simon. Broad shoulders leaning against the French doors, he simply watched her.

"Simon? Is it bad?"

"Depends, Angel." He didn't sound angry but there was a tightness to his mouth. And the fact that he'd called her Angel instead of Anya or Ms. Raawal in that formal tone of his...helped her draw a breath. "I tried to contact you but you weren't picking up."

"I don't usually check my cell phone when I'm at the last stage of production. They know what it's like," she said, pointing to the four gazes shifting between her and Simon, all of them having clearly registered his nickname for her. "Why were you looking for me?"

"Because I think you and I should deal with this. Just the two of us. Not the entire damned world." The dark look he sent her older brother might have felled a lesser man.

Vikram simply glared back at Simon.

"Anya, we don't want to interfere in your private life. Your brothers just want to know if everything's okay, that's all." Naina's soft, calming voice couldn't hide the thread of curiosity beneath or the warning she was issuing her husband. "To reassure themselves that this latest social media stunt hasn't upset you."

Anya flushed as she realized she'd walked halfway up the suite toward Simon. As if he were her true north.

She was not all right. Her knees were shaking and

there was already a cold sweat breaking out all over her skin. She was close to falling apart. "I don't care who's here, Simon. Will you please…" Her breath turned choppy as a ghastly thought stuck her next. "Is it…to do with Meera?" she asked in a soft whisper, covering the distance between them. "Do they know about her? Oh, my God… I promise you I didn't tell anyone. Not even my family. How did this…? How is she? Does she hate me?"

Simon's hands clamped down firmly, reassuringly on her shoulders, pulling her out of the spiral. "No, sweetheart. She doesn't know. No one knows," he said, an instant softening in his eyes. "Only you and me, Anya. Not anyone else."

A shuddering exhale left Anya, but the shivers continued. She wanted to drown in the depths of these eyes, wanted to burrow into his heart and stay there.

"Why didn't you tell us that you were…seeing him?"

Vikram clearly still had a PhD in overprotective nonsense. Still, Anya could see the real worry in his eyes. "I'm not seeing him so much as… Wait, how do you even know that?"

"So you *are* dating him?" Vikram pounced on her.

"Simon, what exactly happened?"

"Someone caught us on a cell phone. Kissing on the bench in Ustadji's garden. The pics are all over the damned internet."

Pushing away from him, Anya fished her cell phone out of her handbag and typed in her own name in the browser. Something she never ever did. Ever. Pictures of her and Simon—three different angles—of her sitting across his lap, plastered to him while they were lost in a passionate kiss, his broad palms all over her back, her arms clinging around his neck…

Her gaze moved over the write-up, her heart in her throat.

Anya Raawal's secret affair with Simon De Acosta!

Apparently Anya Raawal—the usually reclusive member of the powerful Raawals—has cracked the code to get to the rich, successful Simon De Acosta: building a friendship with his daughter Meera Verma.

It's no secret that the two have been spending a lot of time together on the set of Raawal House's latest production. Their unusual friendship had been noted by more than one team member. Looks like clever Anya knew all along that the way to the property tycoon's heart is through his daughter…

Her phone slipped from her hand and fell onto the carpet with a loud thud. "They make it sound so bad. As if I befriended her to get to you, as if I…" Tears knocked at her throat. "Meera…has she seen this? Did she ask about it? Please, Simon, what did you tell her? Did you tell her it's not like that? Does she hate me now? What should I…?" Her knees gave up and she sank to the floor.

"Shh…breathe, Angel." Simon's deep voice cut through the loop. A mere second later, he was there, weaving his arms around her. He pulled her into his lap as easily as if she were a child. Muscled arms hugged her; a warm mouth bussed her temple until all she felt was him.

And still, the spiral of her thoughts continued.

Did Meera hate her now?

Would she never want to see her again?

Would she lose her baby girl already?

The thoughts were like tips of poison poking at her and she struggled to draw in a breath. Her chest felt like there was a large rock pressing down upon it.

"Look at me, Anya. Look at me." Simon's voice was pure possessive demand and Anya automatically followed it. Let him tug her out of the dark hole.

Dark eyes captured hers and held. His fingers gripped her jaw firmly, his breath coating her skin in warm strokes. "Tell me three things, Angel, three things you can see and smell and touch."

"You," she said, tears pouring down her cheeks, "I see you." She rubbed a finger over his brow. Over the dominating sweep of his nose. Over the tension lines around his mouth. Her chest rose and fell on a shuddering breath. "The scent of you is in my pores and I like it…" She stroked her hands over his broad chest, the thick nap of his sweater cool and soft under her fingers. His heart thudded under her palms, his muscles clenching at every touch. "I can feel you… And my hands can't get enough."

But the panic was like a monster waiting to swallow her down given a moment's thought. She raised her teary gaze to his, desperate to make him understand. "You know it wasn't like that, Simon. I would never use any child like that, especially not her." A sob fought to break through her words. "I would never use you to get to her either. I…hate how the media can ruin things like this… I hate how they corrupt everything."

His arms were like a vise around her shoulders now. "I know that. Look at me, Angel." He was a shimmery vision through her tears as Anya tilted her face. His brown eyes were full of trust, his mouth rising up at one corner in a familiar gesture that stole her breath. "I know you, Anya. Trust me right now if you can trust nothing else."

Something in his tone beat away at the spiral, as if he were truly her knight. Her hero. Anya bent her head, burying her face in his neck. She counted to ten, breathing in the male scent of him. "What does she think of me now? What did she say?"

"She saw the posts, yes. In fact, she was the one who said I should call you. That you wouldn't have seen it. That I should talk to you, warn you, before someone else told you."

Anya laughed through her tears, her words a blubbery mess. "Meera is so precious, Simon. You should be very proud of her."

"She is and I am. It was you who reminded me that she has a solid head on her shoulders. She doesn't believe any of the trash they wrote about you using her to get to me. I asked her if she wanted to talk about it, and she said she wants to talk to us both. In her words, she's dying to get all the gossip from you. She's fine, Anya, I swear. Look at me."

Anya looked at him—at the face of this man she'd

propositioned for sex, the man she'd blurted out her most precious truth to, this man she'd accidentally proposed marriage to in a moment of madness. And yet he was here. Whatever she threw at him, he caught her. He held her as if she was the dearest thing to him in the world and he… Her breath fluttered for a whole other reason as she saw her reflection in his deep brown eyes. "I'm sorry for losing it so spectacularly."

He shook his head while pushing away sweaty tendrils of hair from her forehead. "The last few weeks have been a lot, Angel. Falling apart is nothing to be ashamed of."

"I did my best to see you where we wouldn't be interrupted, Simon."

"Hush, I know that. If someone's been irresponsible, it's me. I'm the one who turned that discussion into something else, the one who kissed you in public. I'm the one who didn't see how much Meera was worrying over me. I didn't realize how tuned in she was to my own emotional state. You…made me see that."

"So maybe we could say we're rescuing each other?"

One corner of his mouth tilted up. "You could say that."

"You know my idea that you should marry me is beginning to sound better and better," Anya blurted out too loudly, intent on lightening the mood, wanting to tease him.

The atmosphere in the sitting lounge shifted into something else then, the tension ratcheting up even higher than before. There was no chance her brothers and their wives hadn't heard that remark.

Anya closed her eyes and cringed.

Simon's quiet laughter shook his arms and shoulders and her body. She opened her eyes to see him shaking his head.

"I'm so sorry," she mouthed, loving the wide smile curving his mouth. Loving how he shielded her from even her family's gaze until she was ready to face them.

"No problem. This will give me a chance to take on your older brother."

She gasped. "God, please no. Don't give him a reason to dislike you, Simon. Any more than he probably already does," she said, lowering her voice now when it was too late.

She pushed back from his warm embrace, even though she didn't want him to let go. Pushing onto his feet in a smooth move, Simon pulled her up. Anya swayed, but only for a moment. Fishing out a tissue from her handbag, she wiped her face and turned to face her family.

The concern in her brothers' grief-stricken faces, the shock in their tight mouths, brought fresh tears to her eyes but she held them back. God, all the years she'd hidden away, all the years she'd refused to live her life to the full, she'd only compounded their guilt. "I'm sorry you had to see that. But I'm fine. Really, I am," she said.

Virat studied her and Simon before saying, "Meera, is she our—"

"Yes," Anya said, cutting him off. "But I don't want to talk about that. I don't want even a whisper of it leaving this room. I don't ever want Meera to be hurt by any of this. She's our first priority." Something she spied on her brothers' faces made her soften her tone. "It's enough that I know her, that I can see what a brilliant girl she is. Enough that she knows me too, and that she considers me a friend."

They all nodded. Whatever flicker of sympathy and worry there had been two seconds ago in her brothers' eyes turned into a flare of pride. But of course, she should have known her older brother wouldn't stay quiet for too long.

"You can't marry him just because he is…her father," Vikram said, coming to stand by her side. "We don't know anything about him."

"And how do you plan to stop me, bhai?" Anya said, at the same time that Virat said, "It's her life, bhai. At least, she's finally living it."

Vikram's scowl disappeared. He regarded Simon with fresh eyes. "For one thing, don't you think he's… too old for you?"

Anya looked at Simon. His expression curious, he raised his shoulders, as if saying, "This is all yours." But he didn't remove his hand from her shoulder, to remind her he was right there with her. As if they were part of a team already. His quiet strength at her back made her feel as if she could take on a mountain. "This from the man whose wife is twelve years younger than him," Anya said, winking at Naina. And for all the years he'd tormented her with his overprotectiveness, she added, "Old or not, he serves my purpose. Believe me, I've already taken him out for a test drive."

Simon laughed again, sending vibrations down her

spine. It was deep and from the belly and the most wonderful sound she'd ever heard.

Now both her brothers looked like they wished they'd never had to hear that. Had never provoked her into saying it.

"Good for you, Anya," added Naina while Zara whooped and the three of them burst into laughter. Her brothers watched her, mouths agape.

"As much as I loved seeing your sister putting you both in your place, we're not actually getting married. That was never under…consideration," Simon said diplomatically.

How could she not like him when he tried to save her pride, save her face even with her own family? How could he not see how irresistible his kindness was?

"Anya has more than proved to me that she has nothing but Meera's happiness at heart. Meera and she have already grown close. I ask that you stay out of this. I would not have you hurt Meera in any way with your interference. Even if she's your…" He never finished the thought. But he regarded Anya for a second and added, "Or Anya, for that matter."

If her brothers thought it wildly out of line that he was warning them to be careful with their own sister, they didn't bat an eye. In fact, she thought she saw a glint of respect dawn in her older brother's fierce gaze.

Like recognizes like, Anya thought, with a roll of her eyes.

"But now that our… *Meera* knows about whatever it is between you two, or some version of it," Vikram said, "where does this go?"

"That is for Anya and me to decide. And for you to go along with, whatever our decision," Simon said, his statement nonnegotiable and delivered just as bluntly. It was clear Vikram had met his match in Simon.

"You're okay with all of this?" Virat asked her, and there was more than one question in there. There was concern and worry but there was also faith in his eyes—in her. In her capabilities. In her choices. In her strength to keep standing through this.

Overcome by a sudden impulse, Anya hugged both her brothers. They'd long taken the role of her guardians, thanks to their parents' neglect and far too public marriage problems.

Her older brother especially had had all of her family's financial burdens thrust onto his shoulders when he'd been barely eighteen. "Yes, I'm good. I mean, it was really hard when I saw her for the first time…but I'm dealing with it well now. I can do this, bhai."

"I can't believe I didn't realize that Meera's that baby girl I held all those years ago." Vikram held Anya's wrist, his face wreathed in pain. "I'm sorry I didn't do more to keep her in your life, Anya. I'm sorry that I had no other choice but to urge you to give her up—"

"No, I'm the one who should beg for forgiveness," she said, for once able to see the past clearly. This talk had been long needed. For all his faults, Vikram had always looked out for her and Virat, who were several years younger than him. And in return, all he'd gotten was resentment from both of them. "I resented you so much for so long and you didn't deserve any of it."

Her oldest brother squeezed her shoulders until she

fell into his arms. "You don't owe me anything, Anya. I know I'm pushy and arrogant sometimes, but I've always only wanted the best for you and that sweet baby. You were so fragile when you were carrying her, and that was before you lost so much blood after the delivery…all I wanted was to protect you as much as the baby."

She looked up and the awful guilt in his eyes, perversely, made her stiffen her spine. "I didn't understand for a long time how much was on your shoulders back then, bhai. You were trying to dig our finances out of a hole by revitalizing the Raawal House of Cinema, and at the same time trying to get Mama and Papa to behave and keeping Virat out of trouble. And through it all, you looked out for me. You looked out for that baby girl when I couldn't, when no one else would."

She wiped her tears and smiled. "And now…have you seen what a beautiful, brave, talented girl she's grown into? Have you seen what a wonder she is?"

When he nodded and smiled through his tears, Anya went up on her toes and kissed his cheek. "I'm sorry that I never thanked you. For myself or for finding such a loving family for her. So I'll say it now, bhai. Thank you for looking out for me. Thank you for looking out for my baby. I was not ready in shape or form to be a mother." Anya swallowed the lump of grief in her throat. "You made a hard decision and you became my villain. But you never wavered. I can't thank you enough for that."

Tears in his own eyes, her brother wrapped those

long arms around her. There was no need for words as they stood like that for countless minutes.

Anya sighed, feeling as if another wound that had festered for so long had finally begun to heal.

Feeling as if the past had loosened another painful claw from her present.

Feeling free and whole and light for the first time in years.

CHAPTER SEVEN

"I'M SORRY YOU were pulled into all that family drama," Anya added, feeling awkward in the suddenly empty suite. Her brothers and their wives had left and for the first time in...forever, Anya felt as if she were a new person. A different person.

In a way, she felt relieved that they all knew. They knew what Meera was to her. And they knew that, whatever the future held for her, Anya could look after herself. For the first time in years, she'd come out of her shell and she was taking up space in her own life.

And they knew that Simon cared about her.

She wasn't going to delude herself that it was anything romantic or even close to love, but the fact was that he cared about her. Just as she did about him. And she held that knowledge close to her heart like a lick of flame giving out constant warmth in even the darkest patches of night.

"I wish I could say I don't understand where they're coming from. But I do." Simon rubbed a hand over his face. "I know how it feels to see a loved one suffering and be powerless to help. How...it eats away at you.

How it makes you seem harsh and unyielding when all you're doing is trying to help."

The little glimpse into his past sent a shock through Anya. She wanted to know everything about him—about this man who had a great capacity to love, clearly, but didn't want to.

"Simon, what are you talking about?"

His gaze was distant. "Rani... I didn't always give her what she wanted. And she resented me for it."

"How...how do you mean?"

"Let's just say I let her down. Especially when she needed me."

His revelation startled Anya. From everything Meera said, she'd assumed his marriage had been perfect, his wife a paragon of perfection she could never compete with. And yet, he sounded as if he blamed himself for Rani's unhappiness. How? Why?

Curiosity gnawed at Anya, but she was loath to intrude. Especially after her family had just done so in such a spectacular fashion. "I can't believe that you would ever have hurt her, Simon. What did you refuse her?" When his jaw locked tight, Anya tried to pick up the thread of their conversation. "I...never realized how hard it must have been for bhai back then. How heavily it weighed on him that he couldn't do more for me," she said, pointing her shoulder at the closed door behind her.

"You weren't much more than a child yourself," he said gently. "I can understand Vikram's helplessness even better now. His need to hover around you." He handed her a bottle of water and she took it gratefully. "You look tired."

She felt her gaze on her face as she tipped it up and drank it in one long gulp. "I was working straight for three full days. That might have triggered the panic partly too."

"Does it happen a lot?"

"Not frequently anymore. I haven't had an episode since the night I discovered who Meera is and before that it was some years ago."

"But it happened a lot after you…gave her up?"

Anya nodded, squeezing the bottle of water in her hands. "Before too."

She didn't like thinking about that period of her life at all. It was like a nightmare waiting to sink its claws into her again. But she wanted to share it with Simon. She wanted to put it to rest finally.

"I was sixteen when I met…him. We used to meet in secret. I badly needed an escape and he provided it. Outwardly, my family was the uncrowned royalty of the industry. But it was all hollow inside. My dad's gambling habits and Mama's three gigantic investments into reviving her career meant we were close to being bankrupt. They'd already ruined Vikram and Virat's childhoods with their constant public breakups and reunions. And Vikram…he was trying to hold it all together, trying to keep Virat from running away. My grandmother did her best to look after me. And this man…he gave me sweet words and false promises."

Simon's fingers rested on her wrist, as if to keep the ache of it at bay.

"I didn't even know until I was too far along that I was pregnant. And then when I did find out I hid it from everyone. It became this strange obsession I began to focus on. That man was long gone. Especially after I told him that our wealth was nothing but a smoke screen." Anya rubbed at her eyes. "Sometimes I see Meera and I think… God, how naive was I to just fall for a predator like that?"

"From everything I gather, you didn't have the easiest childhood. The tales of your parents' escapades are still talked about now. It's not a jump to believe you were looking for some attention and fell prey to the wrong guy. Meera, on the other hand…"

"Has had the most wonderful upbringing. And she has you uprooting your life and moving to another country just so she could try her chance at acting. If I ever decide to have a child again, that's the kind of…" Heat climbing her cheeks, Anya let the words fly away from her lips.

"Shouldn't you consider that before you throw proposals willy-nilly at the first man you like?"

Anya tried to not take his brusque tone personally. "What do you mean?"

"That you should know what a man can give you and can't give you before you propose." He sighed and closed his eyes. "Rani and I lost entire years trying to conceive. She went through so much, mentally and physically. Our relationship never quite recovered." She saw his Adam's apple move, as if the admission was still painful. "You should know, Anya, marriage and children and love…those aren't things I believe in anymore."

Her heart thudded at the flatness of his words. He wasn't simply warning her away. There was a well of pain in his heart. "I didn't mean to bring up painful memories for you." She cleared her throat, trying to make her way through the tension between them. "Simon, about having a child… I was daydreaming. Until you…and Meera came along, I never gave a thought to the shape of my future. I had no particular dreams."

"When did you tell your family about the pregnancy?" he asked, cutting her off.

Anya wanted to push the issue. Tell him what she'd realized in the last three days. That she'd take a casual affair with him in the present. For however long it lasted. Especially now that Meera knew a version of the truth about them. But the tight lines around his mouth made her back off.

"I didn't tell them," Anya said, picking up the thread of her own past. "I collapsed one evening—my blood pressure was dangerously high—and Vikram found me. I don't think he or Virat recovered from that for a long time. I know they blamed themselves for not looking after me better."

His dark eyes full of understanding, Simon simply listened. And for him, because she wanted him to know this, Anya went on. Just this one time. "I got medical attention after that but things really didn't improve. My body and mind felt so…disconnected. And I went into a very deep depression."

"And after you gave birth?"

Anya sighed. "That was another disaster. I lost a lot of blood and nearly went into a coma. Vikram spent the weeks leading up to the due date talking to me about adoption. Promised that he had a friend who'd reassured him that the baby would go to parents who absolutely wanted her. He spent hours and hours with me, telling me I was too young, too unwell. That it was a responsibility I just wasn't ready for, and that I needed to look after myself first.

"I finally relented—especially after the doctor told us that it was going to be a difficult birth. I held her for a little while, looking at her darling little face, but I was still hemorrhaging so they had to take me away."

Simon clasped her hand in his.

"When I became conscious two days later, she was gone. That depressive episode continued for a long time. For years, the only thing I remember feeling was this…irrational anger toward Vikram. But he never held it against me."

"So you're saying I should give even more credit to the far-too-full-of-himself Vikram Raawal?"

Anya smiled, her heart warming up at the fact that that's exactly what Simon intended to do. "His heart's always been in the right place."

His thumb traced the plump veins on the back of her hand. "I'm glad he looked after you. What you went through…was incredibly hard. Rani would've wanted me to thank you for giving us such a wonderful gift."

"It didn't feel like that at the time. I didn't even have

time to bond with her properly...it felt like my heart was breaking."

He nodded, his deep brown eyes searching for something in hers. Before Anya could figure out what it was, he let her hand go. "Thank you for sharing that with me. I can't imagine how painful it must be to talk about it."

His words felt formal, practiced, as if he was establishing distance between them again. As if he needed to pull back from the intimacy her shared secret had suddenly woven around them.

"What are we going to tell her?" Anya asked, feeling super tired but determined to get this over with. "Should we say I had...kind of a breakdown and you had to play my knight in shining armor? That it wasn't romantic so much as an obligation? That you..."

He scowled so fiercely that she clasped her elbows in opposite hands. "What?"

"There's no obligation between us, Anya. Sooner or later, she's going to realize that I'm insanely attracted to you."

Simon wanted her. Maybe even with the same desperation that she wanted him. But he clearly wasn't happy about it. In fact, sometimes Anya got the feeling that he was downright angry that it was *she* he'd found himself drawn to.

She didn't understand that. Because not once had he ever hinted—by word or gesture—that he didn't like her. That he didn't respect her.

After dealing with emotionally closed off men— her father and even her brothers to an extent—for most of her life, Simon's openness and honesty was like a breath of fresh air. And yet…the more he learned about her, the more he seemed to want to pull away.

Slowly, he extended his hand toward her face, as if he didn't want to spook her, and waited. Only when she nodded did he clasp her cheek in his broad palm.

Holding his gaze, Anya leaned into the simple touch. Her breath stuttered as the pad of his thumb rubbed back and forth. Again and again. He didn't lean in or pull her toward him, didn't turn the touch into something sexual. Neither did he let her go. For long minutes, they stood like that, her thigh leaning against the side of his. Her lungs full of his woodsy scent.

She wrapped her fingers around his wrist. "One day you push me away—" she nuzzled her face into his palm, loving the rough abrasiveness of his skin, learning the length and breadth of his blunt-nailed fingers "—the next…you're holding me through a panic attack and threatening my brothers to watch themselves around me or else."

His brows pulled into a line. As if he was realizing only now how his actions could be perceived. "Kindness and decency don't make me into a suitable romantic partner for you. I think that's what Vikram was trying to tell you."

"And yet, those are the qualities I rarely find in most of the men I know." Releasing his palm, Anya rubbed her hands over her hips. She had to give them something else to do. "Also let's not forget sex appeal," she teased. "That really clinches the deal for me."

His laughter thrummed through her spine, pooling low in her belly.

"I shouldn't have distracted us from the topic of what we'll tell Meera."

"I won't make you look weak to her just so we can get out of a sticky situation. You never needed rescuing, Angel. Not even the evening we met."

"What did I need?"

"Someone to simply stand by your side. Someone to remind you that you'll come out of that too."

Anya wondered if he could hear the thud of her heart, if he could see in her face that she'd fallen in love with him at that moment. Just a little. "You want to tell her the truth then? That how we met was as strangers screwing against the wall?"

"Damn, you're blunt when you're angry."

Anya shrugged, enjoying the dark strip of color at the crest of his cheekbones. The man's face was full of rough planes, and broad strokes. As if the sculptor had stopped midway because he'd realized this face was better off raw and unfinished.

"I... I'm not ready to talk about my questionable decisions with my daughter. I might never be ready."

Anya pouted. "Just so you know, I'm officially taking offense at being called a questionable decision. That's the meanest thing you've ever said to me."

"I will present you with a more appealing term then."

"Simon, what if I were to make you a different kind of proposition? One that could both distract the media and also give us lots of mutual orgasms along the way?" She had no idea where her boldness was coming from. While she wasn't desperate for just any man, she wanted to live. She wanted to have fun, she wanted more pleasure, she wanted to share more moonlight kisses with him.

God, she'd done enough hiding for one lifetime.

Interest gleamed in his eyes and she felt as if she was going to float away on a high. "You think you could handle a purely sexual relationship?"

"I'm thirteen years younger than you, old man. Our generation is all about the casual. And for the sake of the complete honesty that we've both always engaged in, I won't know if I can handle it unless I try it, right?"

He let such a filthy curse fly that her battered confidence soared. A strange knowing fluttered through her heart, however much she tried to deal with rational facts. That their fates were tied together. And by more than Meera. There was a reason the universe had pushed her into Simon's path. A reason Simon had wandered out into that corridor instead of ignoring her distress.

She just…had to have faith in it. And in herself.

"So…what's your answer? Do we put on a fake relationship for show, or am I allowed to touch you for real?"

His mouth curved into a lazy smile that drew grooves around his mouth. "You're quite bloodthirsty beneath all that fragile softness, aren't you, Angel?"

Anya pouted. "I mean, I understand not accepting my ridiculous marriage proposal but if I'm forced to suffer through a bout of celibacy, especially when I'm the most horny I've ever been in my life, then yes, it's going to make me feel better if I can punish you for it."

He dipped his head, as if to hide his expression. "Why do I have the feeling even your punishments are going to be enjoyable?"

"I'd hate telling Meera any kind of lies, Simon."

He clasped her cheek, his expression gentle and yet somehow consuming. "Then we'll tell her the truth."

"Which is?"

"That we like each other." A glimmer of smile broke through and she felt drenched in its warmth. "But that neither of us is in a hurry. That we're just simply exploring what might be. That should work until the shoot gets wrapped up."

"Okay," she said, leaning her forehead against his shoulder. "You think one of us will be ready to move on by then, don't you?" Anya prompted, wanting to know the truth.

He shrugged.

Anya sighed. "Will you promise me that—"

He broke her off with a hard, fast kiss to her lips that sent her blood pumping despite her exhaustion. His forehead rested against hers, his breath warm against her skin. "Nothing that happens between us, or doesn't happen will affect your relationship with Meera." He traced a path under her eyes with the pad of his thumb gently. "You look shattered. And that was before you saw the news."

"I feel it," she said, giving in. "It's always like that during the week rushing to rehearsals or the shoot. I'd like nothing more than a bath and then to crawl under the sheets."

"Sure you won't fall asleep in the bath?"

The question made her flush. "I don't think so."

He tapped her cheek. "Okay, go get out of these clothes. You have to take better care of yourself, Anya."

"Sir, yes, sir," Anya threw behind her shoulder, warmth blossoming in her belly. She didn't doubt for a second that Simon was extra concerned right now after witnessing her panic attack. But still, his care felt like a childhood blanket wrapped around her. They'd had sex and yet, there was a true intimacy in the small things, in everyday life that she wanted more of. "I will do my best to satisfy you."

She heard his laughter behind her and her own mouth curved into a broad smile. Just talking to Simon—even about the most painful part of her past—made her heart sing, her body thrum. When she came back to the bathroom in a thick, fluffy robe that barely covered her thighs, the bathtub was filled with hot water, the scent of jasmine oil rising up from it coiling through the air, with a few candles lit up around it.

Simon stood at the door, his gaze firmly staying on her face. "Don't fall asleep in there, Angel. We have connecting rooms. I'll be back to check on you."

"Connecting rooms?" Anya said raising a brow. "Whose idea was that?"

"Mine." From the wicked light in his eyes, he knew exactly what she was thinking.

"So you knew how this was all going to play out?"

"The second I saw the headlines, yes. I knew how

it would affect you and I planned to keep you close." He waited, as if worried he'd find complaints from her over his highhanded behavior. "That was before I realized your brothers would interfere. I didn't want you to think you were alone in dealing with this...just because I..."

"Just because you rejected me?"

"I rejected your ridiculous proposal as you called it. Not you."

Anya walked toward the bathroom and came to a standstill in front of the door. "Ahh...that means I'll just have to find the right angle to tempt you."

Surprised delight shone in his eyes. "If you don't want me to see you naked, Angel, you better get out of the bathtub fast."

"And you think that's going to make me get out quickly or stay in for longer?" She looked at him wickedly over her shoulder, her fingers lingering on the knot of her robe. "You're confusing reward with punishment, Simon."

She had the ultimate reward of seeing his eyes darken before she closed the door on him and leaned against it, her knees shaking.

Who'd have known the Raawal boldness would come in so handy one day? And she was only getting started.

CHAPTER EIGHT

SIMON FOLLOWED ANYA'S voice to Meera's room across the corridor and pushed the already-open door ajar. If they were not on the production set or the rehearsal halls, he would always find Anya and Meera together either at the small cafe in the neighborhood village or in one of their rooms.

In the two weeks they'd been in Udaipur, the three of them had already settled into a routine. Despite the unpredictability of a production set in progress, delays in schedules, problems with supply chains, somehow Anya made it easy for not only Meera but for him to find some kind of stability.

Much as he wanted to, Simon couldn't deny the fact that she'd made herself indispensable to both of them and not for any selfish agenda of her own. Not for any other reason than the fact that she cared about Meera and him.

He'd seen her work ten to twelve hours each day, coordinating last-minute fittings and repairs based on rehearsals of the fight scenes, redesigning a part of the men's armor because some of the leather belts had been lost in delivery, and still she always made time for Meera in the evening.

Every small thing Meera needed, from help with rehearsing her own lines to dealing with a fever on the very night when Simon had been out of town for an overnight trip, dealing with his daughter's first heartbreak—apparently the punk light boy had found a girlfriend in the catering company—Anya was ever ready, with infinite patience and calm demeanor and quick-witted answers that satisfied even the sulky teenager that Meera could sometimes be.

As he watched her move around Meera's room picking up all the myriad things his daughter scattered about, a tight knot emerged in his chest. He forced himself to exhale, forced himself to examine the source of his tension.

He'd been waiting for a break in that soft, generous smile.

For a fracture in her sunny temper where she'd say she needed a break from Meera or him or both.

For the dream to lose some of its shine in the dirty patches of reality.

For her to get restless or bored or annoyed…which, he knew, would've been completely fair. What struck him was how he'd been comparing her to Rani and that was unfair to both women. For all he'd assumed she was fragile, Anya had her feet solidly on the ground.

If Meera was busy with something, Anya asked Simon if he wanted to have dinner together. If she was going on a day trip to play tourist and visit local spots on the one day Virat had decided he didn't need her, she asked him if he'd like to come along. If Simon happened to be working late—which he mostly had to because he still hadn't completely decided if he wanted to make Mumbai his new HQ—she dragged in her portable sketching table and her box of pencils and loose paper and worked alongside him in silence.

While Vikram's PR manager put a tight quality control on what was leaked from the movie production site by the crew, a few pictures of him and Anya had made it to the social media sites. After the first baseless rumor, apparently, the media and the public were now quite fond of him and Anya as a couple.

And despite his resolution that he'd not send her mixed signals, that he wouldn't take advantage of her generosity, Simon had complied with most of her suggestions. Basically, because—for all the lies he told himself—there was no one else he wanted to face over the dinner table. No one he wanted to chat with whether it was about Meera's future or art, or even his own business.

The woman was driving him out of his mind, just as she'd promised she would. And after just spending an entire day in Thailand, bored to death at meetings and parties, Simon had begun to question why he was denying himself this spot of happiness and pleasure.

"Oh, God, Anya, do we have to go through this again?" Meera whined, bringing his attention back to the scene in front of him.

Dressed in a loose skirt and a shirt that she'd knotted below her breasts, Anya was taking Meera's measurements. The groove of her spine bared by the shirt

called his gaze every time she moved. "We didn't actually discuss this, Meera. I simply mentioned it to your
dad and you. Before either of us could decide, you went
ahead and okayed the interview."

Meera did the whole "rolling her eyes and blowing
a pent-up sigh" routine. "I heard Vikram sir tell you
that it's better to get in front of this, instead of letting
the media drive it. And Virat sir said he agreed."

It was Simon's turn to sigh. His daughter had a huge
crush on both her uncles. Thank God she thought any-
body older than twenty-one was gross.

"Yes, that's true," Anya said, her tone still worried
but firm. For all her unconditional love for Meera, she
never let the teenager treat her like a pushover. "But
my brothers conveniently forget that they've spent their
whole lives being the media's darlings. And they're
men so they've always been given more leeway." Anya
sighed. "Not that they didn't have their own challenges.
I'm just saying they…don't know what it is to be a
young girl who's unwillingly thrust into the limelight
and is measured against her illustrious mother whether
she wants to compete or not."

Meera stilled, her eyes wide in her face.

"I don't mean to infer that your…mother was anything like mine," Anya said hurriedly.

"I know," Meera said, her eyes full of understanding that felt far too mature for her age. "Okay, let's go
over everything ready for the interview next week. On
the condition that you'll let me wear the Louboutins
Zara di gave you for your birthday gift."

Anya's eyes widened. "I haven't even taken them

out of the box, you greedy girl. Plus they'll be too big for you."

Meera wiggled her foot in front of Anya's face. "I checked. I'm almost the same size as you. Also, we have identical-shaped feet."

Her hand on Meera's foot, Anya stared. A shadow crossed her face before she recovered with a big smile. "Fine. You can wear them. Once."

Meera threw herself at Anya with a whoop and almost sent them both toppling to the floor.

With a strength he wouldn't have guessed she held in her slender form, Anya righted Meera and herself and they settled safely on the floor and leaned against the bed.

Simon stayed at the door, unwilling to interrupt the scene.

"They'll ask about working with my brothers," Anya said, her tone serious. "They'll dig for stories about your mom. And just when you're relaxed enough, when you think you're doing well, they'll pounce with a question about me and…your dad."

"To which I'll say my dad's single, Anya's adorable and it's nobody's business," Meera said with a teenager's confidence that she could storm through every obstacle in her life.

"They'll almost certainly ask what you think about having me as your stepmom." Before Meera could reply, she continued. "I'm sorry that we've put you in—"

"My dad's happier than I've seen him in a long time, Anya. Why are adults so…thick?"

A deep sigh gusted through Simon. His daughter had gotten to the punchline far faster than he had.

Her mouth falling open, Anya seemed taken aback by Meera's confident announcement. "I grew up with parents who didn't care how their antics in public affected us. So if you're upset, that's perfectly valid."

"Anya, for the last time, I'm not upset."

"Okay. That's good. Because I'd hate it if you were."

"And I'd never think you're trying to replace Mama. If you do marry Dad, we'll be more like…friends."

Anya frowned, as if realizing that she was fast losing control of the situation. "Please remember we told you that—"

"I knew something was going on between the two of you long before anyone else," came back Meera. God, his daughter had a smart mouth on her. "Even before you were caught smooching in public."

Cheeks pink, Anya spluttered. "First of all, we weren't smooching in public, we thought we were alone, and second of all…" Anya seemed to have realized what she'd betrayed for she slapped her hand over her mouth. "This is inappropriate."

"I agree. Now if only that stunt master who keeps flirting with you realized he's got no chance against my dad." Pride dripped from that last sentence.

Simon pushed the door open, unwilling to swallow his curiosity. Unwilling to just watch from the sidelines any longer. "Who's this guy hitting on my girlfriend?"

Meera squealed and threw herself at him. "Dad, you're back."

He kissed the top of his daughter's head, while his

gaze met Anya's over it. A soft pink crested her cheeks, her eyes wide and beautiful. "I finished the meeting early in Thailand. So who's this guy?"

"Oh, he thinks he's a total stud, Dad," Meera said, rolling her eyes. "But don't worry. Anya only has eyes for you."

"Hey," Anya protested, throwing a scarf at Meera, that fluttered to the ground midway. "Stop spying on me for him."

"Well, neither Dad nor I want to lose you and everything's fair in love and war."

Simon laughed. "So much for your trust in your old man, huh?"

"I don't know how it was done in your generation, Dad, but in this new era," Meera said cheekily, "you actually have to spend time with your woman if you want to keep her. Especially someone as hot and in demand as Anya."

When Simon would've swatted her on her shoulder, she slipped away from him with a grin. "Now, I have to be off before Virat sir bites my head off again."

She was off and out of the room, like a storm, leaving a tense silence behind. Simon closed the door and clicked the lock into place. He stood leaning against the door, watching Anya as she collected the assortment of papers and clothes they'd strewn around.

"How long is she going to be out this afternoon?"

"Rehearsals and then archery class and then stunt practice…at least three hours."

"Good."

She sucked in her breath in a soft gasp.

"Are you into this…stunt master stud?" he asked into the silence.

Frowning, she looked up. "No. I don't change my mind about who I want in a matter of days."

"Is he bothering you?"

"Not at all. I think he's more in awe of Vikram than he is genuinely interested in me. He keeps asking a thousand questions about him. He's awkward and clumsy, even worse at flirting than I am."

"And yet he's poaching on my territory?"

She raised a brow, her chin tilting up. "What am I? A pheasant for him to steal?"

"What you are, Angel, is…mine," he said, loving the taste of it on his tongue.

Without waiting for her answer, he walked across the room and locked the connecting door into his room.

Then he went to the king bed, sat down on her side and proceeded to remove his shoes and socks. He pulled his dark gray shirt out of his trousers and undid his cuffs. He unbuttoned his shirt all the way through and then, only then, did he look at the quiet woman still sitting on the floor.

"Come here." Now that he'd decided he wanted her, his control was hanging by a thread. For all that she'd boldly asked him to go to bed with her, he knew how inexperienced she was. He didn't want to spook her by showing how desperately he needed her, didn't want to scare her even though all he wanted was to devour her whole.

Her teeth bit into her lower lip. Her gaze landed on his chest and then skidded away. "How did the trip go?"

Feeling devilishly wicked, Simon shrugged off his shirt completely and went to work on the waistband of his trousers. He'd never been more thankful for all the hands-on construction projects he took on, for his body had remained lean and fit. "As well as could be expected."

He'd undone the button on his pants when she whispered, "Simon?"

"Hmm…yes, Angel?"

"What…what are you doing?"

He gave her his hand, and she took it. Pulling her up, he tugged her until she fell into his lap. "I'm calling myself all kinds of names."

Her fingers landed on his bare shoulders. Then boldly moved downward. The smattering of hair on his chest seemed to consume her attention for she ran her palm up and down his chest, her mouth falling open on a soft gasp. If she felt an ounce of the pleasure that coursed through him, he didn't blame her. "Why?"

"Because I went to a meeting in Thailand when all I wanted was to be inside you."

Her hand stilled, her gaze colliding with his. "Oh."

He grinned and took her mouth in a hard kiss. "I would like to formally accept your proposition, Ms. Raawal."

A cute little frown tying her brows, she raked her nail across his nipple. He hissed and hardened against her bottom and her eyes widened. She wriggled, the wily minx, and his erection responded by showing its eager appreciation. Her words were a raspy whisper across his skin. "I've made you so many propositions,

Simon. Which one is it that you're accepting?" Bending her head, she licked a path from his neck to his nipple before she flicked the flat bud with her teeth.

His self-control dissolving like a mist, Simon launched her backward onto the bed. He was on her in seconds, his substantial weight held up on his elbows. Her legs fell away instantly, forming a welcoming cradle for him. He let his hips fall, grinding his erection into her sex. His eyes rolled back in his head when she chased his hips with hers with a needy groan. "This proposition, Angel."

Head thrown back, she arched into him. Her fingers gripped his biceps, and she pushed her head up to meet his lips. With a raw groan, Simon let her tongue into his mouth. She seduced him with her tongue, with soft nips, with hard licks, until he was grinding on top of her like a teenager.

With one hand, he pushed up the flowing skirt she wore, loving every inch of the silky-smooth skin he discovered with his fingers. He bit back a curse when he found a flimsy thong, already damp with wetness. He bent his head and kissed the pulse racing at her neck.

"Angel?"

"Hmm…"

"I need you now."

"Okay, yes."

"I want hard and fast and…"

Fiery pink coated her cheeks but she nodded. "Yes, okay. But then after, slow and lazy."

He grinned and licked her lower lip. "You sound like you have your priorities all set."

"I have a list I've been composing, Simon. All the things I'd do to you, with you, if I ever got my hands on you."

"Yeah?" he said, pushing the thong away, wondering what kind fate had dropped her into his lap.

"Yes. If you have anything you want to add to the list, just let me know."

Holding himself off her, Simon pushed his trousers down. His erection jerked up into his belly, hard and already beading at the tip.

Her gaze wide, Anya traced a line down his length. Up and down until all he could hear was his own heartbeat in his ears. Then her finger rested gently on the soft tip, before dipping into the drop of his release.

And while he watched, his tendons jutting out with pressure, she brought the finger to her mouth and licked at it. Her gaze when it met his was darkly carnal, wicked and full of delight.

"God, this is going to be over before we've even started if you look at me like that, Angel."

"I want to lick you here, all over," she said, fisting his shaft. Moving it up and down with enthusiasm if not expertise.

Simon thrust into her hands, blind need driving him. The thought of that lush mouth wrapped around his erection pushed him that much closer to his release. "Some other time," he managed before he used his free hand to push away the flimsy thong. Gently, he traced the lips of her sex before dipping his finger at her opening. Wetness coated his fingers. She was ready for him, so ready. "Now, Anya?"

"Yes," she said, thrusting her hips up.

Taking himself in hand, he covered up with a condom and thrust into her wet warmth in one go. And didn't stop until he was all the way inside her.

The tight clutch of her sex was the sweetest torment he'd ever faced. Her gasp sent a flutter through his nerves, making him impossibly harder inside her.

Simon kissed a path up her neck to her mouth. "Did I hurt you, Angel?"

She turned to him, her eyes dark with desire, her nostrils flaring. Her fingers moved from his hips to his buttocks, her breathing shallow. "I have imagined your weight bearing down on me so many times, Simon. Of having you move over me. So give me more of you."

A pang went through his chest and he shook his head. "I'll crush you."

"No. Please, Simon."

He let her feel a little more of his weight. Her feet wrapped above his buttocks, her thighs stretched wide. A feral grin curled her lips and he kissed her deep and hard, taking more than giving.

Then he pulled out and thrust back in. Her head moved up on the bed and she wrapped her fingers around the headboard. "Do that again, but faster."

"Hell, you're ruining me, Angel," he muttered before he gave her what she wanted. What he needed too. But he didn't want to go over the edge without her. "Undo that knot. I want to see your breasts."

Breath falling in sharp staccato, she complied with his demands. He roughly pushed away the flaps of her shirt and her bra. Her dark brown nipples were plump, her pulse fluttering away at her neck.

With her hair in disarray, her clothes still on but baring everything to his gaze, she was his fantasy given life. He bent and licked and sucked the nipple into his mouth, each moan and thrust of her body sending a tingle down her spine.

Then he took her hand from his abdomen and brought it to the swollen nub at her core. Her eyes wide, she looked down at the erotic sight of his fingers holding hers, pressing, caressing, flicking the tight bundle of nerves. "Keep that up, Angel," he whispered, praying he wouldn't disgrace himself. "I want to feel you clench around me, Anya. I want to feel everything my body does to you. And keep your eyes open."

With the raw command, he upped the tempo of his thrusts.

Their gazes held as he used her hard and fast, the intensity of their building climaxes, the thud of their hearts, telling them it was going to be even better than last time.

That the remaining few weeks weren't going to be enough. That there was nothing casual about this at all.

Soon, pure pleasure overtook any rational thought and Simon roared as her climaxing muscles milked him hard and tight and he fell apart in her arms.

He held her long after she fell asleep.

It shouldn't have been this easy. This simple. She shouldn't have been able to sneak into his head, his thoughts this easily.

But she was there, without question. She made him

laugh. And she made him want. And she made him...
realize how lonely he'd been for a long time. She made
him realize that he'd sort of given up on himself too.
But he wasn't sure if he'd ever have the courage to trust
his heart again.

Or trust himself with her happiness.

CHAPTER NINE

IT WAS PAST eleven when Simon knocked on the connecting door between his and Anya's four days later. Again. Nothing but silence answered him.

While she hadn't told him herself, Meera had let it slip that it was Anya's birthday. Simon couldn't wait to see her face when he revealed the small surprise he'd planned for her at the last minute. It had shocked him, his overwhelming desire to do something for Anya, his own excitement while he'd arranged the surprise, the depth of his need for it to be something special. As special as her smile, her joy she so easily shared with him and Meera.

But today of all days, he'd been stuck in meetings for hours and when he'd finally returned to their suite, both Anya and Meera had been gone.

After waiting for more than a couple of hours, he gave up on the pretense of work. He wouldn't be able to concentrate anyway until he knew Anya was safely in her bed. Or his, where they'd been spending the last few days. Every moment they could manage, like young lovers stealing away from adults.

In their case, it was any time they were afforded by Meera's and Anya's rigorous schedules. At forty-three, Simon wasn't into instant gratification nor should he have the stamina for it, but God, Anya made him feel wild in his skin again. After that first lazy afternoon they'd spent in bed, after which they'd both fallen asleep together, he'd wondered if he was going through some kind of midlife crisis. If that was the reason Anya appealed to him so much.

Just the question had left a horrible taste in his throat.

However many reasons and excuses he'd tried to explain away the madness in his blood, this wild obsession with her, nothing fit.

It was just all her.

Her laughter. Her sensuality. Her generous heart. Her…unending energy to try everything she claimed she'd missed out on for so long. Her sweet, soft body that she gave without inhibitions even as he pushed them both to the edge and then careened right over it.

How long would it last though? How long before Simon let her down too?

Feeling far too restless in his skin, he pushed up from his seat and pulled on a sweater. He'd simply walk to the set. Vikram had security guards posted all over the location and through the walkway between the site and the luxury hotel where Anya, Meera and he were staying but he still felt a thread of anxiety in his gut when she wasn't back in her room.

Just as he was used to worrying over Meera. It had

no rational basis; he knew that much. And he didn't right now care beyond that.

He heard the laughter and shouts before he entered the makeshift tent that had been erected for the crew to rest during outdoor shoots on hot days. Bending his head to get through the low arch, he walked in to find a center table decorated with cake and candles and balloons. There were almost fifty crew members circulating with drinks in hand.

Simon was about to ask Vikram—he and the older Raawal had made peace of sorts—when he saw the flash of a smile and an elegant hand with a leather strip in it that he knew was Anya.

She was standing with a young, brawny actor—the same so-called stud that Meera had talked about before. Simon knew because he'd gone on set the next day to find out. The man clenched his arm so that his muscled bicep was on glorious display while Anya was checking the leather thong on the arm straps that were part of the costume.

Every time he flexed his bicep—and he did it a few times—the strap loosened and Anya tried to buckle it up again. With a laugh, the actor pointed to the same kind of bands he wore on his wrists, ankles and even thighs.

It was the first time in his life that Simon felt the taste of possessiveness and jealousy curl on his tongue.

"She's not as fragile as she looks."

He'd been so immersed in watching Anya that he hadn't even realized that Virat had walked up to him. "I know that."

"Then why do you look at her with such wariness in your eyes?"

Simon stayed silent for a beat too long to deny it.

Apparently, Virat was more discreet than his brother for he didn't push Simon. "I've never seen Anya this happy. This…excited about life in general. Her work has reached a new level of brilliance. I never did believe in the whole 'suffering creates better art' nonsense."

Simon swallowed his token protest and waited. He hadn't even realized he needed to hear this. Hadn't realized how deep and raw a wound Rani's silence and her unhappiness and her retreat had carved in him.

As if sensing this, Virat continued. "I can't tell you the number of years Vikram and I spent trying to get her to celebrate her birthday in a big way, to coax her out of her shell. And yet, this year, she ordered the cake and balloons for herself, and she invited the crew. She's even invited our parents when she usually tries her best to avoid them. I think my sister's finally celebrating who she's become."

Simon could see the joy written plainly over Anya's face. Something that made his own chest expansive and full. "That could have been to do with finding Meera again."

Virat turned to face him and Simon was forced to do so too. As much as he liked to keep the Raawal brothers at a distance—the reason being how protective he felt about not only Meera but Anya too—he'd discovered in the last fortnight that he genuinely liked both men. For all they'd been born with silver spoons and a legacy, they had also borne a lot of burdens along the way and had hearts of gold. Their choice in wives spoke most volubly for both of them.

"You and I both know that's only half the reason, Simon. Neither Vikram nor I can overlook the fact that you made the hardest thing in her life easier for her to face. That you've been supportive and kind during every step of the way for Anya. I can't tell you how grateful we are to see her this happy, and to see Meera flourish."

His heart felt as if it might explode out of his heart. "I only want Meera's happiness. And… Anya's."

"And yet you still doubt that it lies with you?"

Simon said the words that had been sitting on his chest like a bag of rocks for days now. Even weeks. "Anya has been through a lot already. She's told me about her anxiety and I've seen her panic attacks. She's still so young and—"

"And you think that somehow makes her less of a person?" Virat bit out, jaw tight. "Did I mistake you for a better man, Simon?"

"Of course it doesn't make her any less. She has so much to give despite everything, such fire and courage…don't think for one second I don't see her as she really is, Virat." Simon searched for the right words. "But you have to understand that I… The thought of having her happiness in my hands, the thought of hurting her in any way…the very thought of being the reason Anya loses out on something she truly deserves…" Simon hated speaking the words aloud but he did it anyway. He needed the reminder these days. "I hate to agree that Vikram's right, but I am older than her and there are some things that my life experience has taught me to be wary of. Some things that I'm incapable of giving at this point in my life. I'm jaded and at the risk of sounding like a quitter, I'm not sure I'm the right person to deal with…fragile things. That young show-off, as much as I hate him pawing at your sister, is probably a better man for her than I am."

"No wonder my brother likes you so much beneath all the bluster he aims at you… You're both cut from the same overprotective, overthinking cloth." Virat looked at Anya, who'd clearly noticed them chatting and was heading their way. He bent forward and gripped Simon's shoulder hard. "Don't undercut her like that. Not when she's just found her wings. There's nothing more arrogant than assuming you're responsible for someone's happiness. Especially when it's the woman you just admitted to seeing and admiring. Don't coat your cowardice, your fears with her imagined flaws, Simon. Believe me, I did that once, and I almost lost Zara."

Simon stared at Virat's retreating back, his words reverberating through him.

Was it arrogant to believe he would become responsible for Anya's happiness if he took this any further? Was he doing her an injustice thinking he knew better for her than she herself did? Was he wrong about the state of his marriage to Rani there at the end too?

He scrubbed a hand down his face just as Anya tapped him on the arm. "Hey. Is everything okay? Did Virat say something he shouldn't?"

Simon faced her and shook his head. "No. I think I

got a dose of why the critics call him a blunt but brilliant filmmaker."

She didn't look convinced but she nodded. "What are you doing here? Meera's spending the night with Zara's sister who's visiting. I checked on them again before I came down."

"I came to find my errant girlfriend."

The bright shine in her gaze went straight to his head. "Yeah?"

"Why didn't you invite me to the celebration?" he said, waving an arm in the direction of the cake and the balloons.

"I know how much you dislike hanging out with the movie crew. I didn't want to force you to do it after-hours too."

He tapped a finger on her scrunched nose, wanting to touch her again. In many more places. In a spot where they weren't surrounded by gorgeous young men and their brawny bodies.

"How many times are you going to have to fix that joker's armbands and thigh bands and calf bands? Have you wondered if maybe he's breaking them on purpose so that you will admire his bulging biceps and fix them for him again?"

For a second, Anya blinked, confusion apparent in her eyes. And then she laughed. Loud and bold and drifting up from her belly. Her already-wide mouth widened and her too-big nose flared and she was so beautiful that it stole his breath.

At some point during her laughter she'd tucked her arm through his and leaned against him. Simon tried to remind himself that she was probably only doing it for the avidly watching crowd. But he knew that was a lie. Just as it was a lie that he had wrapped his other arm around her because it was the gentlemanly thing to do when she was clinging to him.

Simon knew most of the heads had turned toward them under the marquee now. Not surprising because they'd gathered to celebrate Anya. Also not surprising because, while they were meant to be a couple, neither of them had embraced in public. Her brothers and sisters-in-law and even her parents—all of them were staring with such shock in their eyes.

Reaching out with her hand, she pushed a lock of hair from his forehead. "Are you jealous of that muscly actor, Simon?"

"A little," he admitted. "No. A lot, actually."

Something stirred in her liquid gaze. And this time, it went straight to his shaft.

She patted a hand over his chest, as if she was dusting something off his sweater. But he knew she wanted to feel the thud of his heart. As if she knew its beat was already rushing in his ears anytime she was near. "Don't be. He can't handle me."

Simon knew she was half joking but he wanted the answer anyway. He wanted to hear it in her words. "How do you mean?"

Her smile didn't quite disappear but she sobered. She knew exactly what he was asking. "Do you think he'd have asked me what I needed when I fell apart after seeing Meera? Do you think he'd have held me, kissed me, made me feel alive at the worst point of my life? Do you think he'd have shown such care when I told him I'd got pregnant and given up a baby when I was a teenager? Do you think he'd have given me a second glance if I weren't the Raawal brothers' sister?" She pressed against him, her arms going around his neck just as soft music burst through the speakers. Stepping onto her tiptoes, she whispered at his ear. "Do you think he'd see beneath the pretty shell and the wealthy accessories to the real woman with her anxiety and her flaws and her tainted past, Simon?"

His hands went around her waist as if they belonged there and Simon pressed his mouth to her temple. Her confidence and her words resonated through him.

They swayed slowly to the music. The minx knew that he was putty in her hands.

Simon pressed another kiss to her temple. "Happy birthday, Angel." Most of the attending crew had turned away from them.

"I know what I want from you."

"Anya…" he said, injecting a warning into his tone. Her "marriage proposal" had become a running joke between them. Every time he tried to corral this thing between them into some semblance of a temporary affair, Anya teased his retreat by asking him to marry her.

The joke was on him though. Because marriage in itself was not what bothered Simon. He had no idea when it had happened but tying himself to Anya for the rest of their lifetimes didn't bother him at all. He would give her that if it guaranteed her happiness. If it meant he'd never let her down as he'd done with Rani.

But no such guarantee existed in the world.

She lifted her gaze to him and bit her lower lip. "You won't accept even on my birthday?"

He softly pinched the curve of one hip in his hand. Loving the tight dip of her waist and the flare of her hip. Neither had he missed the fact that she'd filled out a bit in the last few weeks. Since he'd first seen her. She'd lost the gaunt look and he liked her even better like this—healthy and thriving and happy.

She gasped softly. "Fine. I was going to settle for a few kisses and one orgasm."

Simon swallowed. Desire and laughter were twin ropes, tightening in his lower belly, curling his muscles tight. He wanted to tell himself he was too old to separate lust and liking, but it would be another lie to add to the pile he was telling himself. "Hell, woman, you're killing me."

More people left the tent, leaving only her family around. Simon held her through two more songs, more than content to just touch her. And hold her. It was enough for his heart to know that she was his.

"My brothers… I trust wholeheartedly. But Papa and Mama… I'm not ready for them to meet you and muddy this up, Simon. Why aren't you rushing me away like a frantic lover?"

Simon raised a brow and she giggled. "This was your celebration. I don't want to hurry you away from it. Especially after Virat reminded me you don't often do this."

Surprise flitted across her face.

For once, Simon wasn't sure what she was thinking.

"I appreciate that you didn't invite me because I'm not a huge fan of the industry." Her eyes big in her face, she nodded. He rubbed his thumb over his cheek. "But you and Meera are a part of this world. I'm more than happy to support you both when you need me to be here."

Simon didn't realize how it sounded until he said the words. But neither did he want to take them back.

She tugged at the collar of his shirt, her mouth trembling. "You're... I..."

"Anya, are you okay?"

She looked at him through a tremulous smile. "I was done a couple of hours ago. All the celebrating I want to do now is with you."

Simon stared at her, another piece clicking into place.

For months before her accident, he'd tried to break through the wall that Rani had pulled up between them. He'd been nearly driven out of his mind trying to work out what would make her happy. About how to build a bridge back to her. Worried about losing her all over again. In the end, her infuriating demands and her silent rejection of everything he'd tried had killed the love he'd once felt for her. Long before she'd decided to go back to acting and try to revive her career, their relationship had died. But then she'd died before she could set her plans into motion.

And here was this woman...who wore everything she felt on her face.

Who asked outright for what she wanted of him.

Who was turning him upside down by her mere presence.

His assumption that she was too fragile like Rani, that she'd fall apart at the smallest obstacle, that she wouldn't know her own mind...disintegrated into dust at his feet.

She was nothing like Rani.

And the realization loosened the tight thread of fear he'd clutched to him ever since she'd set those beautiful brown eyes on him. Maybe Virat was right. Maybe thinking he'd been wholly responsible for Rani's happiness was only his arrogance and worse, his fear talking.

"Where are we going?"

To give herself credit, Anya had tried to bury the question for the entire fifteen-minute ride on the helicopter that Simon kept at the luxury hotel and that he himself had piloted. But it was a little past midnight and she'd thought they'd be in bed.

Instead, he'd tugged her outside, talked on the phone with his arm around her and then said, "Let's go," which instruction she had blindly, happily followed. Of course, he'd asked her if she'd trust him to fly her safely, after rattling off the number of hours that he had piloted for.

Anya stepped out of the chopper now, taking in the restored palace in front of her with wide eyes. She'd studied the history of the city and the kings and queens that had ruled it in majestic splendor. Which was why she knew that the small palace in front of her—small being relative in comparison to the huge, sprawling one that they were currently shooting the movie in— was the only one that had stayed under the ownership of a reclusive royal who'd refused any price tag for the government or any other millionaires.

Clasping her hand in his, Simon simply pressed another quick kiss to her temple before saying, "You'll see."

Anticipation bloomed in her belly as they mounted the steps toward a smaller entrance instead of the grand, wide entrance. A uniformed servant dressed in traditional clothes bowed his head and then bade them to follow. Her mouth progressively fell open as they followed him through corridor after corridor. Priceless art hung on the walls, and there were decadent rugs, and antique furniture casually strewed about the palace. While she wanted to linger and learn the history behind every piece, Anya simply followed along.

After what felt like a ten-minute walk, they were shown into what might once have been a woman's boudoir. For the vast room was covered in mirrors all around her, with several open archways leading into different corridors. Her gasp was loud as Anya walked around, seeing their reflections grinning back at them.

And still, the best wasn't over yet.

Divans of different sizes and heights were placed between the open archways. Each covered with clothes, leather armor, weapons, jewelry.

"What is this place?" Anya asked, feeling as if she was standing at a different time and place in history.

Raising her hand to his mouth, Simon grinned. "It's a private collection. A friend of mine owns it. This palace actually belonged to the famous dancer who was supposed to have been the lover of the king."

"The king who owned the other palace where we're shooting?"

"Yes. Did you know both the palaces are connected through a secret passageway? Although I've heard it's been a century at least since it's been blocked."

"He kept his lover here?"

"Yes. Apparently, she hailed from an enemy clan."

"Or he simply wanted to have his cake and eat it too?" Anya replied, grinning back at Simon.

"Possible," he answered, letting her hand go. "But the clothes and the jewelry and the weapons…they're all centuries old. I thought you would enjoy seeing the collection."

Anya threw herself at him, joy bursting through her chest.

For a second, Simon was stiff around her. Then she heard his laughter and his arms surrounded her. Feeling vulnerable and yet as if she might burst apart, Anya pushed away. "How long do we have?"

"He's having the collection moved permanently tomorrow morning. So I'd say we have a few hours. We can't take any pictures or copy the designs."

"Of course," Anya said, awe filling her throat. "You don't mind if I spend a couple of hours here?"

Simon shook his head. "Be my guest."

After that invitation, Anya didn't hesitate. She let the ornate jewelry, the lavish handmade *lehengas*, the starkly beautiful hand swords and knives dazzle her, carry her away to another time.

It was past three in the morning when she walked up to Simon and told him she was ready to go. This time, no servant walked them out. Dawn was still an hour or so away but the courtyard where Simon had landed the chopper was littered with lights to show the way.

Anya pulled Simon against a wall and kissed his mouth, pouring all the emotion that wanted to burst out of her into the kiss. They were panting when they broke apart.

"What was that for?" Simon asked, his grin wide, his eyes dancing.

"Thank you so much for taking me. For knowing how much I'd appreciate seeing something like that before it forever disappeared into someone's vault."

Simon rubbed the curve of her lower lip, still smiling. "I'll admit to doing it for completely selfish reasons."

"Yeah? What might those be?"

"To win one over all the young studs on the set that keep swarming around you."

Anya laughed so hard that she was afraid her heart might burst out of her. She pressed her face into his neck and licked the salt of his skin. His erection, as if in reward, hardened against her lower belly. "All I want is you, Simon."

With a hard sigh, Simon tugged her toward the chopper, his gaze promising any number of delights.

CHAPTER TEN

OUT OF ALL the things Anya had been terrified that the interview host would ask Meera, she hadn't imagined in her worst nightmare that the thing that would shatter the young girl's easy confidence and expansive faith in the world would be to do with Rani Verma.

With the fact that Rani had apparently signed on to a large project with Raawal House of Cinema—of all the production houses in the world—in what was supposed to have been a huge comeback, a mere three months before her death in the accident. Or the awful rumor that on the same trip to Mumbai, Rani had also visited a high-profile divorce lawyer, according to a source close to the late actress.

Hours later, she couldn't still believe the utter malice in pouncing on a thirteen-year-old and asking her such an intrusive question about her dead mother in what was supposed to have been a fun interview. No wonder Simon hated the thought of Meera in the midst of such a toxic culture.

Her steps felt leaden as Anya remembered the stricken expression in the girl's face.

It had been clear that Meera had had no idea that her mother was returning to Bollywood, or that she had signed on to such a major blockbuster project that she'd have been on a production site for at least nine months.

But Meera had recovered fast, and said it should be no surprise that a talent like her mother's would have come back to the silver screen sooner or later. As for the divorce, she'd said, those were just horrible rumors. Her mouth had been trembling, but her gaze was resolute.

The moment the camera had cut, she had rushed away from the temporary set in search of her father. Anya had followed silently, not wishing to intrude on such a private moment. But wanting to be there in case Meera needed to vent.

For hours after Simon learned of the interview, father and daughter had been behind closed doors in Meera's room.

Anya drifted through the courtyard and then back into the lounge outside Meera's bedroom like a cursed ghost, wanting to go in but so, so afraid that she'd be seen as an unwelcome intrusion. That when it mattered, she'd always be on the outside looking in on father and daughter. Because her foolish heart ached for Simon as much as it did for Meera.

Had Rani and Simon been on the cusp of separation?

Was that why Simon always seemed so reluctant to even broach the topic of his marriage?

I didn't give her what she wanted and she resented me for it... I let her down...

Simon's words pinged through her until useless

thoughts spun around and around in Anya's head. She felt an irrational anger toward a woman she hadn't even known for casting such a large shadow over Meera's and Simon's lives. The moment the thought crossed Anya's mind, she knew she was in deep trouble.

But the truth was that his marriage to Rani—whatever it had been like—cast a pall on Simon's present. Maybe even on his future. On their future. And she wanted to know what she was up against. But she was also afraid of rocking the boat, of pushing Simon when the topic was clearly taboo for him, of losing what little she had with him.

It didn't matter that she'd spent every single night in the last week in his bed. It didn't matter that they'd crossed over all the lines Simon had wanted to draw between them. Her thoughts went in circular directions, her statement that she'd keep it casual biting at her.

After what felt like a long while, Simon stepped out, looking at his phone. His features were taut with tension. Still, a soft smile curved his mouth when he found her standing there.

Relief swept through Anya in waves and she cursed herself for the fear beneath it. Was it fair to herself if she was this scared of things falling apart so easily?

He lifted the phone. "I was just about to call you."

"Is she okay?"

"She's been better," he said, and Anya could have hugged him for telling her the truth. "But she will bounce back."

She nodded. "I want to touch you."

He knew what she was asking. The weary look in

his eyes was replaced by warm appreciation. "You don't ever have to ask."

Anya threw her arms around him and hugged him so hard that she could feel his heart thundering away against hers. It was selfish to think of their relationship in the midst of the heap of hurt Meera was facing but she'd been terrified that he'd push her away. That he'd blame her in some kind of convoluted way. For a moment, she'd forgotten that Simon wasn't that kind of man. "I'm so sorry this happened."

He pressed a kiss to her temple, his own arms tight bands around her. "You're the last person who should apologize. You've been trying to warn Meera and me both that something like this would happen. This is all my fault."

There was such anger in his voice that Anya jerked her head back to look at him.

A thread of fear wound through her heart. "You might not like hearing this but I'm going to say it anyway."

To her surprise, he laughed. A serrated sound that half vibrated with anger. At himself, she knew. He clasped her cheek roughly before he said, "Don't ever change, Angel."

Her heart kicked against her rib cage. At the emotion in those words. At the tenderness in his eyes.

"Tell me," he said, releasing her.

"Rani was so adored by fans and the industry alike that with even a whiff of this news existing somewhere in someone's mind, it was bound to come out."

"So you're saying I messed this up too."

"Did you know she was making a comeback?"

"Yes," Simon said, biting the single word out. "I knew that she had signed with someone but not who. It was her exit plan from our marriage."

The flat tone of his words said more than the words themselves. "Is that what you…fought about?"

A bitter smile twisted his mouth as he held Anya's gaze in a challenge. "You think I'm such a small man as to begrudge her her career?"

Anya's heart ached at the pain etched into his features. "No. I'm just…trying to understand."

Understand you, and what hold your marriage and Rani still have on you…why you look so tormented by this.

But she said none of those things.

"God, I made mistakes enough," he said, his gaze distant, "but I never stood in the path of her career. Not even when it ruined her mental health. We just never got a chance to tell Meera before the accident happened. She wanted all the logistics in place first. She was looking at schools, interviewing nannies… Rani intended to use the movie shoot as the first phase of our separation. She was determined that none of the upheaval would hurt Meera in any way. Whatever was happening in her mind, in her own life, she was a good mother to Meera."

"So you didn't know she'd signed with Raawal House, specifically?"

"No. Nor did she do me the courtesy of telling me that she was considering a comeback before she signed. Our relationship had already…fallen apart when she told me her news. After the fact. I just didn't believe it at first... I was so angry."

For her leaving him?

Had he still loved her when she'd left him?

No, from the first moment, all she'd heard in his voice was guilt. And he was too honorable to play with her if he still loved Rani.

Anya touched her fingers to his arm, gently shaking him out of his reverie. "Then it was bound to get out, Simon. At least now we can look at it this way—the worst is over. If we can just get Meera through this... they can never do anything more to damage Rani's memory for her."

He rubbed a thumb against her cheek. "God, what did I do to deserve you in my life?"

"I'd like to think we both deserve each other," she said, other words fluttering on her lips. "Not in the usual horrible way it's meant. In a good way."

His smile widened. "I got that." He exhaled harshly. "Meera wants to see you. Will you talk to her?"

"Of course I will."

He pulled her to the small lounge at the end of the corridor, his hand at her lower back. "I've told her that I knew about Rani signing that project. That we'd been waiting to have all the logistics in place before we gave her the news. But that her mother had passed away before that ever happened. All of which is more or less true... And the other part..." His gaze had that far-off look again. "I can't destroy her mother's memory, so I've told her that it was all a lie built off the fact that her mother was returning to her career. I think she wants some reassurance from you."

Anya nodded. "For all she didn't blink when they threw that at her, she's only a girl."

He gazed at her for a while, his thoughts inscrutable, his fingers never not touching her in that way of his. Her shoulders, the nape of her neck, her back, his broad palms stroked her. Anya let the touch soothe her, aware that that's what he was doing too.

Then he pulled her to him with a rough groan, and kissed her. Hard. Long fingers buried in her hair tipped her head up for his pleasure. His teeth nipped at her lower lip, and when she opened, he swooped in with his tongue, stroking, licking, until their breaths were a harsh symphony. It was possessive and rough and feral and Anya reveled in every moment of it.

He leaned his forehead against hers, his breath choppy. "I've wanted to do that all day."

Anya licked her lower lip and gasped, the tiny sting making the pleasure singing through her body all the more potent.

Simon's gaze followed the movement. His breath feathered over her in rough strokes. "Damn it, Angel. I'm sorry I was rough."

Anya rubbed a finger over his lush lower lip and shook her head. "You've never done anything with me that I didn't enjoy thoroughly, Simon."

"For once, I don't want to share you with Meera. I want you for myself. I want to forget this entire day happened. I want to bury myself deep inside you. I want to run away from all this…" His arm wound around her waist and tugged until she was pressed against him. Her breasts felt heavy, achy when he crushed her to him. "And you would be the perfect escape. The perfect place to land, Angel."

Anya buried her face in his neck, the raw admission spreading through her limbs like molten honey.

Only an escape, Anya. You're just a temporary pleasure for him. Not a partner he'll share his hurt with, his life with, the nasty, doubtful voice inside her head whispered, but she shushed it up.

When he released her, she said, "I'll ask Naina and Zara over after we're done talking. Meera loves hanging out with all of us." She hesitated a beat and then asked, "Where will you be?"

"I'm going to get drunk and maybe punch one of your brothers for not vetting that reporter enough. For not telling me that it was their house Rani had signed on with."

Shock made her mouth fall open until Anya realized he was joking.

"Don't worry. I'm aware that I'm looking for someone other than myself to blame. But they should serve my purpose for a little while."

"They can take it," she said automatically, her head full of a hundred questions.

"All joking aside, I do think Vikram could have dropped a small hint to me in our conversations."

"And you?" Anya asked, despite knowing that she should let him go. "Have you ever recovered, Simon?"

Instant tension swathed his features, the tender lover of moments ago all but gone. "From what?"

"From the fact that your wife saw a divorce lawyer and didn't tell you?"

He laughed bitterly and thrust a hand through his hair. "Remember how you asked me if I could turn back time that first moment we met? I wish I could, because damn it, I'd have made better decisions. First I hurt Rani and now, what I drove her to, is hurting Meera."

With that, his gaze turned to the dark night beyond the balcony. He'd kissed her, held her, he trusted her to look after Meera, but it was clear that he wasn't going to share his deepest pain with her.

Before she begged him to explain why there was such guilt in his eyes, Anya forced herself to walk toward Meera's room. He didn't need her probing into that wound right now. Didn't need her to bring up the guilt and pain that twisted and pulsed beneath every word.

At least with Meera, she knew that she'd be able to allay her fears, to show her how much she loved her.

Orange light was filtering through the sheer silk curtains in her room by the time Anya returned to her room. While she'd caught more than a few hours of sleep in Meera's queen bed, she felt bone-tired and lethargic like never before. Either she was getting anemic again—she made a note in her calendar to call her GP—or her body was telling her to slow down.

She had been pushing too hard this last month so she'd informed Virat that she was taking a day off and then turned her phone off. After finishing a quick shower, she put on one of the T-shirts she'd stolen from Simon, and crawled into her own bed when she heard the connecting door open with a soft creak.

Simon's broad shoulders and tapering waist and those long legs… She drank in the outline of him as if it was her life's fuel. All the tiredness fled her body just like that, a nervous energy, a restless hum under her skin taking its place.

"I'm awake," she whispered, afraid that he would turn around and walk out.

The night lamp came on by her side of the bed, illuminating him completely. From the dark wet gleam of his jet-black hair, it was clear he'd just showered too. Dark circles straddling his eyes made it clear that he hadn't slept a wink.

Her heart ached for him.

"I'm not drunk."

"It's okay if you are."

"If you want to sleep, I'll leave."

"No, stay."

He watched her from his great height, his brows strung together as if he was trying to solve the mystery of her.

With a soft sigh, he sat down by her side on the bed, his long legs thrown in front of him. For long seconds, he stayed like that, his head buried in his hands.

Anya turned to her side and pressed her hand to the outside of his thigh.

After a few more minutes, he took her hand in his and kissed it with such reverence that she felt heat pricking her eyes.

Scooting closer to her on the bed, he ran a thumb around her eyes. Her nose. Her mouth. The hollows under her cheeks. "Did you catch any sleep at all?"

She shrugged. "We watched a movie until midnight, then she slept. I left a note saying that I'd see her in a couple of hours."

Using his hand as leverage, she pushed up until she was leaning against the headboard. When she pulled, he came closer until he was sitting next to her and she could lean her head on his shoulder. Holding his hand close to her chest, Anya started talking. "She'll be okay, Simon. The fact that I pestered her so much over the past week about the interview I was able to point out that they weave all kind of nasty lies from half truths."

"Thank you," Simon murmured without turning back to look at her. He was staring at a picture of Rani and Meera on the nightstand that the young girl had pulled out of her backpack only three days ago to show Anya.

"Stay with me," she said, sensing his retreat again. Sensing the dark pain from earlier gathering into a cloud about him again. "I wasn't feeling well to begin with this morning. If you leave me now—"

That got him to move like nothing else had. Turning toward her until his broad chest and his handsome face filled her entire field of vision, he said, "What happened?"

"Probably just anemic again. I'll see my doctor soon." Her heart thudded at her daring but Anya made the demand anyway. "Right now, all I need is you. Get ready for bed."

Other than the languid curve of his mouth twitching, he didn't point out her demanding tone. When he started to pull off his V-necked T-shirt, relief swept through her. She shivered as he gathered her hair into one hand and lifted it. Then his warm mouth was on the nape of her neck, his stubbled jaw rasping against her skin. She jerked when he gently bit her there.

"Have you been anemic before?"

"On and off since I gave birth," she replied in a hoarse whisper.

He nuzzled into her shoulder blades and spoke so softly that she almost didn't hear him. "This is the last thing I want to hear right now."

Anya blinked. Worry lines around his eyes deepened. "What...what do you mean?"

A huge sigh pressed his chest to her back. "I've got too many things on my mind already. I don't want to worry about you too."

It was almost as if he was talking to himself than Anya. But it only pushed at the roiling pot of her own emotions. "I'm capable of looking after myself," she pointed out, stiffening in his arms. Had he any idea how hard every word of his landed on her? "I've done it for almost a decade and a half now, Simon. Even with two brothers who think they know better than I do."

Glancing down at her, he frowned. "It's not a reflection on your abilities, Angel."

"No?" she said, challenging him.

"No. I... I used to think you were fragile but I was wrong," he murmured.

"I can be both fragile and fierce, Simon. Believe me, one doesn't negate the other."

He dropped a hard, long kiss on her lips. "I know that." His right hand moved from her neck to her belly and then his fingers played with the hem of her T-shirt in a motion that only served to inflame her senses. "This needs to come off."

Swallowing down the thick desire in her throat, Anya murmured yes. She loved it when he got demanding like that. When he shed his laid-back, easy-going layer and took what he needed from her. When he let the guilt and whatever else gripped him go and immersed himself in this, in her.

It was strange how she'd gotten so used to doing the most sexual things with him, but this...this raw demand in his voice, the small intimacies he demanded of her—like always wanting skin to skin when they went to bed, making her spell out exactly what she wanted him to do, making her give voice to the darkest fantasies she'd never thought she'd want—made her heart beat faster as much as anything else.

Because she saw a Simon no one else knew. Because with her, he was exactly who he was beneath the guilt and honor and the clutches of the past. He didn't have to be a dad, or the grieving widower or the man who'd worn a shroud of loneliness for so long.

She barely had to lift her chest before he had the T-shirt off her.

He turned her malleable body until her back was to

his chest—hard, warm and taut. The hair on his chest rasped against her smooth skin, the hard ridge of his abdomen a shock against her lower back before he adjusted her to his liking. Her bottom was tucked tight against his crotch, and she could feel him hardening, lengthening. Anticipation turned her mouth dry, her limbs shaky, her sex damp and ready.

But he didn't make a move. He didn't tell her he needed to be inside her like he usually did. In the middle of the night. At the first light of dawn. Once, with her face pressed against the ceiling-length glass windows which gave her a view of the courtyard but showed nothing to the people on the other side. Everything he suggested, Anya got addicted to it.

One corded arm wound around her while the other ended up between her breasts with the tips of his fingers resting on her pulse at her neck. Sometimes, his thumb would rub her lower lip; sometimes, he'd signal for her to open her mouth until she was sucking and nipping the pad of it. Sometimes, he'd take her like this, pushing into her from behind, setting a lazy rhythm that made her very blood molten.

He did none of those things today.

Anya felt as if she was being cocooned in the warmest of blankets even as his hard body around her stoked a fire in her lower belly. His mouth rested at her temple. She closed her eyes, willing her heartbeat to slow down.

Maybe the man didn't have sex on his mind tonight.

But she did. And she wouldn't know until she told him. She wasn't going to sleep until he'd rocked her to an orgasm. Until the stress and uncertainty building to a crescendo in her head had an outlet in the form of physical release.

"Simon?"

"Hmm?" His warm breath coated her cheekbone.

"Are you sleepy?"

"Not really." But his tone made it clear that the last thing he wanted was to talk. "Are *you* sleepy, Angel?"

"Nope."

"Tell me what's on your mind, sweetheart."

"Ever since I woke up, I have this…restless hum under my skin. Like this knowing in the pit of my stomach."

He pressed a kiss to her bare arm, humming into her skin. "Like dread? Like something bad is coming?"

That he didn't laugh at her made her fall in love with him a little more. A little here and a little there and soon he was going to own all of her heart. "Not bad or good. Just a…big thing."

"What did your astrology app say?"

"It said this next period was going to be all about change and growth and…whatnot. I thought I'd seen it all already." With Meera and you, she didn't have to say.

"Are you scared?"

"A little."

"What can I do to make it better?"

His rough palm cupped her bare breast, the thumb and forefinger lazily circling the already taut nipple. Fire breathed out from where he touched through to her limbs.

"I…" Anya arched into him, begging him with her body. Begging him to give her what she needed.

"What, Angel?" he growled.

Anya gripped his wrist to stop the mind-numbing circles and thrust her nipple into his palm. A sultry groan ripped out of her as his thumb rubbed the plumply dark bud in butterfly strokes. "I'd like you inside me," Anya whispered, turning all kinds of pink. "As soon as you can manage."

Raising himself on an elbow, he kissed her mouth. Naked want shimmered in his eyes. "I admit to sneaking in here, even knowing you'd be tired, hoping I could do just this. Especially now that there's not a lot of time to spare."

Anya moved to her back and searched his face. "What happened?"

He played with a lock of her hair. "Meera and I are going to leave at three o'clock tomorrow. I mean, today."

Anya wondered if he could feel the small fissure that had cracked across her heart. Would it always be "Meera and I"? Was she always going to feel like an outsider when it came to them both?

Never "Meera and us" or "you and me and Meera." It was irrational how much it hurt.

"When were you going to tell me?" she demanded, before she could curb the words.

"I did just now."

"Where are you going?"

"I have a meeting in Seychelles. I thought it would be good to get Meera out of here for a while so I'm taking her with me. So that the two of us can spend some quality time together." He drew a line from her neck to her belly button and then back up again. "I talked to Virat and Vikram. They looked at her call sheets and were able to move some dates. Her calendar's free for two weeks. Vikram also told me that he thought I'd known Rani had signed with Raawal but seeing as she died shortly afterward, he hadn't discussed it with me out of respect for my loss. He felt it would have been like rubbing salt into a wound. The information was confidential and he has no idea how it leaked, but he'll be investigating the interviewer's sources."

"Oh, that's good you sorted things out with him. Really good," she said, swallowing the lump in her throat. Two weeks of not seeing Meera or him…it felt like a lifetime.

This isn't goodbye, she reminded herself and yet it felt like that.

"Vikram was feeling guilty enough about the interview, so I pushed my advantage and also got the dates extended for the second project Meera's signed with Raawal House," he continued, unaware of the tumult of her emotions. "This way, she can take more than a year off after this. Decide if she really wants to do the second one. I should never have agreed to the two-project contract in the first place. She was so damned excited, for the first time in months after Rani's death, that I just gave in."

It was clear he was examining all the choices he'd made after the leak about his private life. Making all the necessary routes clear for Meera's exit from the industry, if that's what she wanted. For him and Meera to leave as easily as possible. To move on from this life that he had never really wanted for either his wife back then or his daughter now, even though he'd supported both.

The sensible part of Anya's brain pointed out that this was good for the teenager. So much exposure to what could sometimes be a toxic culture at such a young age, so much pressure to always be at her best in front of the hungry media, her every mistake examined under an unforgiving microscope…it wasn't healthy, despite all the measures Simon could choose to take.

And yet, all she could think of was that it meant distance for her—from Meera and from Simon. All she could worry about was that he was retreating from this world in which she lived because of the news about his marriage. Because a wound that had never fully healed had been cracked open again.

But what else might drive him away from her then?

What could come up that would tell him she was getting too close to him?

And God, was she forever going to wait for that moment to come? Wonder if that heavy burden of guilt he carried without fully sharing might fracture the fragile wings of their own relationship? For all that she teased him, Anya didn't need marriage or promises of forever. She just didn't want to constantly live in fear for their relationship. Didn't want to feed the monster that was her anxiety any more fuel.

A warm kiss at the corner of her mouth brought her attention back to him. "Anya?"

"I think that's a great idea," she said, mustering false enthusiasm. Questions hovered over her lips, demanding, probing, and yet she couldn't give them voice. Not when his wandering hands created pockets of pleasure all over her skin, stole her breath and her mind.

His upper body hovered over her while his fingers fiddled with the seam of her panties. "Virat said you're incredibly busy all of next week."

Anya gave another nod, a small part of her taking that as some kind of explanation for why he wasn't inviting her on their trip. God, she was really clutching at straws.

"Anya, all this has made me—"

Anya pressed her hand to his mouth. "I don't want to talk anymore. Especially if you're leaving in a few hours." Especially if he was going to break up with her.

Maybe she was a coward but right now she didn't want to face her emotions or his decisions. Her T-shirt and panties disappeared and in the blink of an eye, he flipped them both over until Anya was straddling his hard thighs. She'd gotten used to being naked in front of him but with his dark eyes and roving hands, she felt completely exposed right now.

Not just because of how open she was in this position. There was nowhere to hide, no chance he wouldn't see her heart in her eyes. And from the hungry look in his, she wondered if it was exactly what he wanted. If he wanted to take the little she hadn't already offered him yet—the rest of her heart, her love. Her everything.

Any token protest she could have mustered drifted off her lips as Simon cupped her breasts with his hands, and this time, he gave her exactly what she needed. From her neck to her breasts to her belly to her sex, he played her nerve endings like the strings of a guitar. Her spine rose and fell in tune to his demands, her skin so heated that Anya gave herself over to the sensations he strummed through her.

"Bend down, Angel."

Anya did, her body fluid under his command.

His mouth closed over a hard nipple and she jerked at the sharp, stinging pleasure at her sex. One hand on his rock-hard shoulder, she panted. With his other hand, he separated her folds, his fingers feathery and gentle. He stroked her own dampness over her before he thrust first one finger and then two into her.

Even wet and ready, the intrusion speared Anya.

"Look at me, Angel. Open your eyes."

Anya flicked her gaze open to find him watching her with a devouring intensity that brought on a fresh wave of sensation. From that first time since she'd told him she didn't come easily, he'd always given her what she needed. With words—sometimes sweet, sometimes filthy—with caresses—soft and wicked—with his hands and mouth, and fingers and his body.

Pulling out of her, he sent his wet fingers up her bare flesh in an unholy trail, until his finger reached her mouth. Anya opened her mouth and licked it, tasting herself.

"Will you give me whatever I ask, Angel?" he asked in a ragged, hoarse tone that said this was about more than just sex.

Anya licked his finger and released it with a pop.

And for the first time since they'd met, she lied. "I will, Simon."

Dark satisfaction flared in his eyes. Anya heard the rasp of the condom wrapper and then he was rubbing the swollen head of his erection at her center. Flickers of flame went up and down her spine, flooding back down into her lower belly and tightening into a feral knot.

"Ready?"

Anya looked down into his eyes and nodded.

One hand on her hip, he slowly pushed himself inside her. "Don't close your eyes, Angel. Watch this. Watch how you swallow me whole. God, Anya…" His groan as he settled himself all the way in made her shiver.

Anya jerked at how achy and invasive it felt like this. How full he made her feel.

"You okay?"

"You feel so deep like this, Simon. As if you're everywhere." Her back arched of its own accord and she braced her hands on his hips.

"You feel like heaven, Angel." Keeping his thumb on her bud, Simon urged her to find her own rhythm. Heartbeat thundering, skin flushed, Anya used her knees to push up and thrust down in time to meet the jut of his hips. On and on she rode him, gently at first, and then finding the perfect countermotion to his thrusts. And all the while, he told her how good she felt, all the while, he kept that thumb where it was needed, driving her wild.

Soon, Anya was toppling into her climax, his name

on her lips. Pleasure fractured in her lower belly in deep, concentric circles, so acute that tears lashed down her cheeks.

Hands on her waist, Simon pushed up. Then she was turned onto her back while he balanced himself on his elbows and knees, his erection still hard inside her. Even in the languorous haze of her orgasm, Anya noted the flare of his nostrils, the corded strength of his shoulders, the damp sheen on his skin and the... raw ache in his eyes.

"Simon?" she whispered, fear already fluttering through her.

Gathering her hips upward, holding her gaze in guarded silence, he started moving inside her again. His thrusts were hard and short and then he climaxed with a soft grunt. He was instantly off her, even though she loved being crushed into the mattress by his powerful body.

Nuzzling into her neck, he peppered a trail of kisses up her chin and cheek. "You're very quiet."

Anya closed her eyes, afraid he would see everything even now. That maybe it was already too late. Wondering if there was going to be any part of her left that he didn't claim, that he didn't take. "I'm just tired."

And when he wrapped his arm around her and kissed her and held her as if he would cocoon her with his body, after gently cleaning her up, she shed the silent tears that had been building for a while.

This trip he was taking with Meera... He wasn't breaking up with her.

But it had made her own heart crystal clear to her.

And this person she'd become—this woman who could see her daughter and love her but not acknowledge her, this woman who so boldly went after the man she wanted—she couldn't hide from the truth anymore.

CHAPTER ELEVEN

THANKFULLY, SIMON WAS out when Anya bid an emotional Meera goodbye with a quick hug and a kiss. Of course Meera had asked her why she wasn't coming along. Blinking back tears—God, she was leaking tears these days—Anya had said there was no way she could get away from work. Not for two whole weeks.

With fervent promises to chat every day, the teenager had let her leave.

Now, Anya was hiding in the empty studio near the set.

Lunch had come and gone but she'd barely touched the sandwich or the soup. Her appetite had gone from bad to nonexistent this morning and she knew she'd pay with one hell of a headache later but right then, nothing could hold her attention.

Nothing but the fact that time was passing and Simon and Meera would leave, and for the first time in several weeks, she was going to be utterly alone again.

In her head. In her heart. In every way that mattered.

Her astrology app kept spewing some version of "Trust your instincts" and it made her furious.

She just wanted the hours to pass fast. Until she knew, her body knew, that he had left and she could give up on this…strange feverish anticipation coursing through her. When she could go back to her room and hide for the rest of the day. Pushing the sketches she'd been working on aside, she pressed her fingers to her temples when she heard the door open behind her.

Her breath stuttered. She didn't have to turn to know that it was Simon.

"Hey."

Bracing herself for the impact, Anya turned. As always, her entire being came awake at the sight of his ruggedly handsome face. In a white linen shirt and dark denim, he took up all the space in the small room. And all the oxygen. Hope fluttered through her, half keeping her functioning, half choking her. "I thought you'd have left by now."

"Something came up at the last minute, and I pushed our departure back by half an hour."

"Oh… Does Meera need something?"

"No, she's talking to your brothers and sisters-in-law."

Her heart was beginning to pick up pace, the tight jut of his jaw making butterflies dance nervously in her stomach. "Did she forget something?"

His head jerked up, as if she'd shouted at him. "You talk as if Meera could be the only possible reason I'd come to see you."

Gripping the wooden desk behind her, Anya stared at him. "No, that's not what I meant," she said, frowning.

"And yet you would do anything I ask just to be close to her, wouldn't you? Give me anything?"

His question pierced her, again carrying that note of something she couldn't quite put her finger on.

"Anything within reason, yes," she said, trying to inject humor into it but failing utterly. "Simon, what's going on? Why are you angry?"

"Meera let it slip that you might not be here when we come back. Is that true?"

Anya blinked, and searched for an answer. She should've known Meera wouldn't keep it to herself. "I was just thinking that out loud when she brought up our schedules over the next few months."

"So will you be here or not, Anya?"

"Probably not," Anya said, tired beyond measure. "I don't think Virat's going to need me after the coming week and I... I want to get away from it all for a while."

"From Meera or from me?" Anger resonated in the last bit. "Have we become too much for you?"

"I would never abandon Meera like that," she said, hot color sweeping up her cheeks at his disbelieving expression. "Do you truly think me that fickle, Simon?"

"I don't know what to think because you conveniently forgot to tell me your plan to leave, Anya. And I don't believe for a second that it's simple oversight."

"Didn't Meera tell you that I said that she's more than welcome to visit me wherever I will be?"

That only made his scowl deepen, "And me, Anya?" he said, taking a step into the small room. "Would I be welcome?"

"All I meant was that I need to lay low for a while,"

she said, knowing that it was a non-answer. "I usually retreat after…after a big project like this."

For the first time since they'd met, Simon looked at her as if she was a complete stranger. There was a hardness to his mouth that she was afraid was there because of her. And yet, he didn't come out and say what angered him. "I don't believe you. I think you meant to run away and hide the moment my back was turned."

"That's not true."

But the truth hung there between them, waiting to strike out if either uttered a wrong word. He rubbed both hands over his face and groaned—a sound that seemed to be wrenched from the depths of his soul. "If you want this to be over, all you have to do is say it, Anya. I can't bear silences and walls and hiding behind reason. Just…"

"What?" she said, aghast that she'd hurt him.

"I put up with Rani's fluctuating moods for so long, thinking she needed space. Thinking she needed me to be just there for her. Thinking she would eventually come to me. But all that did was breed resentment between us because ultimately I couldn't give her what she wanted. I can't go down that path. Not ever again. So please, just tell me the truth."

"Fine, you want to know the truth?"

"Yes," he said, his focus all on her now. He didn't sound angry anymore. He just sounded tired. "Because that's what you and I have always dealt in. From the first moment we met. Whatever you say to me, it won't affect your relationship with Meera."

"Not everything I do with you is because of Meera,"

she threw at him, her chest rising and falling. "I'm upset that you didn't tell me *before* you made plans to take Meera away for a fortnight. I'm upset that you didn't ask me along on your trip, even though I can't come anyway, so it's totally irrational. I'm upset that you…won't share your pain with me, what haunts you about your marriage."

A shutter fell over his gaze. "Why do you want to know what happened in my marriage?"

"Because I want to understand you, Simon. Because… I see the grief and guilt in your eyes and I wonder if you'll ever let it go. I see you retreat from this, from us every time you think of her or your marriage. Because I'm starting to feel resentment for a woman I didn't even know."

Simon stared down at her. But his mouth gave away his shock. "Rani wasn't a bad person, Anya. She wasn't the sole reason our marriage fell apart. I was the one who let her down."

His defense of his late wife felt like a slap to Anya's emotions. "You keep saying that but not explaining it to me. You keep punishing yourself for whatever it is you think you did and now it feels like you're punishing me too."

Now it was his turn to look as if she'd dealt him a punch. "Hurting you is the last thing I want. I… I couldn't live with myself if I did, Angel. That's the entire reason…" A curse flew from his mouth.

"Then tell me what it is that you denied her. What… did she want, Simon, that you couldn't give?"

"She wanted us to try for another baby. She wanted

to go through IVF, even though it failed the first time and left her body a mess, even though this time she was a decade older and was already unwell. She wanted to have my child and I said no. I refused to even indulge in a discussion. After that, she retreated from me completely. Just put up a wall I couldn't break through no matter what I said or did. And that only sent her into a spiral.

The evening before her accident, she asked me one last time and I... I got so angry I let the resentment of two years rip through. She died an hour later."

Anya stared at him, her heart aching. He was clearly submerged in guilt, in thinking himself responsible for Rani's lack of happiness. How could she ever hope to break through that? How could she continue with him in the present when he was still so caught up in the past?

"Why did you...?" Her question hovered on her lips, unformed, her throat full of a sadness. "I'm so sorry, Simon."

He only stared at her, his mouth set into an uncompromising line. "Now tell me the truth, Anya."

She nodded.

"Tell me that the fact that you might not be here when I get back was just an impulse talking."

"It wasn't."

His mouth tightened. "Tell me that you weren't going to simply withdraw from me without even giving me a reason."

"I can't."

His question when it came was soft and quiet. As

if it was wrenched from the depths of him. "What *do* you want from me, Anya?"

Anya stared at him, his face as familiar to her now as her own. At the rugged terrain of his face, his square chin, his broad chest...

"I want—" she rubbed her chest with her hand, feeling as if the ache there might never go away "—I want you to see yourself as I see you—a kind, decent man who's punishing himself for something he didn't do. I want you to include me in your plans—even the smallest ones—because you can't bear to part with me even for a few days. I want you to take this chance on a future with me, even if there are no guarantees. I want... you to let me love you, Simon, because I do...so much."

Simon simply stared at her, his eyes glittering, his nostrils flaring, his entire body radiating such tension that she thought she should feel it in the air around her like hisses and sparks. Then he glanced away and her heart broke.

And still, she couldn't stop her words.

She pressed a hand to her head, the headache she'd worried about suddenly materializing with a hard pounding behind her temples. "I'm sorry. I didn't mean to put you on the spot like that. Especially when Meera needs you more right now." Her mouth curved into an inane smile as if she hadn't already acted completely bonkers in front of him. "You know the astrology app did say something about endings being new beginnings or some such nonsense. Guess now we both know what I've been so worried about."

"Anya—"

"No, please, Simon. Let me keep some dignity intact." Collecting her portfolio and her watch, this time she shied her gaze away from him. "I'm late for a meeting."

The week after Simon and Meera left, Anya called Zara and begged her to acquire a pregnancy test for her without anyone else being the wiser.

Her period was late.

In the thirteen years since she'd given birth to Meera, it had always been unpredictable and late. But this was different in a way she couldn't verbalize. Of course, there was the fact that she'd gained weight in the last few weeks.

The very day they had left, Simon—half asleep and completely wiped out—had wrapped his big palm over her lower belly and whispered, "I can't tell you how glad I am that you've lost the waif look, sweetheart." His palm had possessively cupped her hip, fingers spreading over the small curve of her belly as if to highlight the fact. Then those long fingers moved up her body and did the same to her breasts before rubbing against her ultrasensitive nipples. "And these, these were my favorite even before they became a little bigger."

The fact that her bras had started becoming uncomfortable should have told her. But she had attributed her increased appetite and weight gain to the fact that her therapist had reduced the dosage of her anxiety medication.

But now, now she couldn't bury her head in the sand

anymore. Now, it was sheer stupidity to not face the fact that was staring her in the mirror.

Thankfully, Zara didn't ask her a single question and Anya also knew she wouldn't whisper a word to Virat unless Anya said it was okay to share. And that Virat, unlike Vikram, would simply let her chew through it all first before he made a big fuss. Not that she could go on for a lot longer without everyone knowing.

And yet, even before Zara handed her the pregnancy test and waited outside her bathroom, Anya knew. She knew what the universe had been screaming at her and she'd tried to blunder her way through—calling it anemia, or dehydration or her body simply doing its own thing.

The two pink lines on the test stared back at her as she washed her hands at the vanity. Her emotions resembled the sheet of instructions she'd wadded up into a ball as soon as she'd opened the box.

She was pregnant, Anya repeated to herself.

With Simon's child.

Her and Simon's baby.

She would be a mother again. And this time, she was strong enough, mentally and physically, to look after the baby and herself, to love the baby as she'd always wanted to love Meera.

Leaning her forehead against the bathroom door, she forced herself to count her breaths slowly. The last thing she needed right now was a panic attack.

The thought of facing Simon after the way she'd blurted out her love without him responding in kind, of telling him that she was carrying his child when he'd made it clear so many times that he didn't want another child, made her chest ache.

He wouldn't blame her for this; she knew that. But he wouldn't be happy either. And his honor, his heart... would force him into only one choice.

Anya shuddered at the thought of marrying Simon just for the sake of her baby. No, she was never going there.

The clarity of her thoughts held off the fingers of panic.

Placing a hand on her belly, Anya stared at her reflection.

However Simon reacted to this news, whatever shape their future took, this baby had been conceived in love. She believed that with her whole heart, with every breath in her. And she would continue to hold on to that.

She'd wanted a second chance at so many things—at love, at making her own family, at another child, at... doing things right. And she had it.

She would love this baby as she'd always love its father. And that was the thing to hold on to, even if the rest of her life didn't fall into a more traditional future she'd never imagined for herself anyway.

But first, she needed time. Time to adjust her expectations, time to strengthen herself, time before she told Simon the truth about this baby.

CHAPTER TWELVE

THIS TIME AROUND, Anya had chosen to hide herself away from the public and her own family at Raawal Mahal.

Once it had been her grandparents' home—a cocoon of love and escape for her and her brothers growing up. The place where she had the happiest memories of her childhood. Now Virat and Zara lived here with their toddler son. And since they were on-site in Udaipur and wouldn't be home for a while, along with Vikram and his family, it was the perfect hideout for her.

Anya had worried that the feel of the house would've changed for her, not that she didn't love all the small changes Zara had made to upgrade it. Instead, Virat and Zara's love and the new memories they were making in their home seemed to have just occupied a space alongside the old ones. And Anya knew that's how true love worked. It made space for warmth and connections and joy amid whatever was broken or damaged before. Right alongside past hurts and unfinished healing.

She loved wandering through the sprawling mansion, talking to the child in her belly endlessly, pointing out the art and keepsakes Raawals had gathered for generations. And she hoped the baby felt the love, security and happiness the walls carried within them.

This time, she wasn't going to hide her pregnancy. Not for anyone.

However, her solitude, she knew, was coming to a swift end. Because as much as Simon had a right to know first, her brothers had figured it out. Even without Anya confirming or denying it. She had, in the end, warned them to stay out of the entire affair between Simon and her if they ever wanted to have an active role in her child's life.

The word *affair* had sounded small and finite in its scope when what she felt for Simon was so expansive that it defied words. There was no doubt in her mind he'd suggest that they marry. But there was also no doubt in her mind that she wanted all or nothing. Even if that meant explaining to Meera why her brother or sister was going to be born out of wedlock and convincing her that Anya wasn't abandoning Meera, that she still absolutely adored her and always would.

Her cell phone's ping brought Anya back to reality.

Every day for the past week, Simon had been texting her. As if they hadn't argued before he'd left. As if she hadn't blurted out like a naive fool how much she loved him only to get no response. Not that she'd change her words or the sentiment. Just their delivery.

She'd been so emotional, like a pressure cooker with no whistle to let off the building pressure. So unbalanced by both the emotional and physical changes rushing into the very landscape of her life.

Instead of looking at his latest text, Anya scrolled up to read the whole lot. As she did several times a day. And twice before falling asleep.

The first text had arrived a week ago just as Anya had settled into a routine at Raawal Mahal.

I'm back in Udaipur with Meera. Which I'm pretty sure you're aware of since she texts you like thousand times a day. She missed you terribly on the trip. I don't know how your generation does things but we're not done, Angel. That was just a disagreement we had. Not a breakup.

She'd laughed first at his lengthy texts, remembering how relentlessly Meera teased him about his perfect grammar. But she loved receiving them. Loved knowing that he was sending them so that she could look at them over and over again. Loved that he'd remembered that she'd told him she hated confrontations. Loved that he was building a bridge between them slowly. Even though he'd admitted that Rani's silences had tormented him.

Loved that she knew her so well. That he loved her so well even though he was so gun-shy he'd probably never admit it.

Her heart had crawled into her throat as Anya waited for more. Mouth half-open, fingers clutched tightly around the phone, she'd finally fallen asleep.

Her phone had pinged around midnight.

I miss you. I miss how you cuddle into me in your

sleep. I miss how you tuck your ice-cold feet between my calves and steal all my heat. I miss the sounds you make when I'm deep inside you. Seychelles was damn cold without you. Who am I kidding? Even blazing hot, Udaipur is cold without you to warm me up. I hope you're looking after yourself. I know I messed up but I'm not giving up on us.

In the dark, the words had blurred in front of her sleep-mussed eyes, before she'd realized that she was crying. She'd wanted to reply like her breath depended on it. But she'd held back. Not because she was angry with him or because she wanted to force some kind of announcement from him. She wanted so desperately to tell him her news. And she just couldn't, not over a text. She knew if she messaged him back, she'd end up blurting it out. She wanted to wait until she could see him face-to-face calmly, rationally, with her plan for her and the baby's future laid out so he didn't have to worry about them.

The next text popped up the next morning as Anya had just finished a session of meditation with an on-line class.

Meera got her first period. She's made it clear that she wishes you were here to help her instead of her bumbling Dad. God, Angel, I need you here. And not just to soothe Meera.

The next morning one more:

I stole a piece of chocolate from the delivery you sent for Meera. So I'm the only one you're still ignoring? You know the only reason I'm not there with you right now is because I can't leave Meera alone, right?

The next day, two more texts arrived:

Even Virat won't tell me where you are. I think I prefer his no-nonsense approach to Vikram's arrogance. Who died and made him king of the world?

You know what's freaking me out though? How weirdly silent Vikram is right now.

Two more texts the next day:

Meera asked me what I'd done to mess this up with you. I told her that her dad was an old coward.

She glared at me and then told me to fix it.

Three more the next day, like clockwork. Simon's texts had become the highlight of her day.

I think I've given you enough space now, Angel.

Zara's offered to look after Meera.

I want to see you. If you think I won't use Meera to find out where you are...you underestimate me.

Finally, Anya circled back to the unread texts she'd received a few minutes ago.

Are you free, Angel? Because I'm close. Actually, I don't care if you are free or not. I'm done trying to tiptoe around this.

Her heart crawled into her throat as Anya heard the front bell ring. As she heard their once oldest servant and now a family member, Ramu Kaaka, open the door. She could hear Simon's voice filtering up from the main lounge, up the stairs and finally his steps outside her bedroom. The fact that Ramu Kaaka had simply invited him in meant her brother—probably Vikram—had given up her location.

Anya had barely a second to brace herself when the door opened and Simon walked in. Into her childhood bedroom where he dwarfed everything all over again. Where she'd once dreamed of a man just like him— tall and kind and so…achingly handsome.

A dark blue sweatshirt spanned the breadth of his chest and Anya had to force herself to keep breathing at the sight of him. From his hard, powerful thighs to the gray at his temples, he was like a fist to her heart. Dark stubble decorated his sculptured cheekbones and his square jaw, giving him a bit of a roguish look.

He said nothing, as if he'd used up everything he had to say in those texts.

His hands went to her messy sketching table and all the free paper she'd left floating around. Head bent, he studied some of the sketches until his fingers touched on one she'd done of him.

She wasn't a portrait artist by any means—not a good one. But it was all she'd been doodling for the past two weeks. The man had a thoroughly masculine face that had drawn her interest from the first moment she'd seen him. Even before he'd asked her if he could help.

He held up another sketch of him, frowned and then he put it down.

Only then—after what felt like the longest three minutes in the history of time—his gaze moved to her. As if he'd needed time to brace himself.

Whatever he saw in her face, his big body came to a stillness. It was like a predator slowing down, all the tense muscles and tendons coming to a standstill. Anxiety rippled through Anya's belly as if there was a swarm of stampeding elephants in there instead of the usual butterflies. Her hand instantly went to her slightly rounded belly, as if to soothe the baby from her swirling thoughts.

Simon's gaze followed her hand and the frown on his face broke into such an anguished expression that Anya felt it like a lash against her skin. "You're pregnant. That's why you've been hiding from me."

Her knees shook under her.

A curse flew from his mouth, filling the air between them. His big body settled into her chair, his face buried in his hands. "There's no rhyme or reason to what the universe does, is there? It's all chaos. And yet you try to make it make sense to you with all those apps and…"

"Simon?" Anya said, a thread of fear winding around her heart.

"The number of years that Rani wanted to have a child, the things she put her body through…"

Anya felt as if she'd been slapped right across her face. "I'm sorry you feel that way. That this opens up your wounds all over again."

He looked up then, as if her apology had ripped him from the past he'd been stuck in. He paled, regret etched into his every feature. "Hell, Anya, I didn't mean for that to sound as harsh and insensitive as it did. I just meant that it's quite a shock."

Anya wanted to move closer, she wanted to wrap herself around him, until his shock subsided. She did nothing of the sort. "I know."

"All those years, all those tests, Rani told me she thought it was something to do with her body but we were both tested and the problem was never conclusive. I didn't… I never realized I could still father a child. You've had weeks to come to terms with it. I've only had a few seconds."

He was right. And she had expected he'd be shocked. Hands wrapped around her midriff, Anya nodded.

"Did you know before we left for Seychelles?"

"I didn't. But I was…definitely not myself that day. Every small thing was getting to me. I thought it was anemia or dehydration or the effects of the change in my medication. I didn't realize until a couple of weeks ago. My periods have always been incredibly irregular."

Hurt pinched his features. "And you waited all this

time? You told your brothers and you didn't tell me?" His voice almost broke on the last word and Anya couldn't stay away from him anymore.

She went to her knees between his legs, her fingers catching hold of his hands. "Simon, I'd never do that. They just…figured it out. I didn't want to tell you in a text. Can you imagine for a moment how I felt? You've made it so clear since we met that you never wanted to do this again. That you were done with marriage and babies and love. I just… I needed time to brace myself before I saw you. I want you to know that this is welcome news for me even if it isn't for you."

He still didn't look at her and Anya thought this might be the cruelest he'd ever been to her. Questions and thoughts came to her lips and swung away, so many of them that it was impossible to pin one down. But before she could make up her mind, Simon was lifting her and planting her ass on the edge of the bed and then moving away.

Hands clasped in her lap, Anya watched as he paced the confines of the bedroom, agitation written into every line of his body. Time ticked slowly in seconds… but her heart was doing its own thing. Finally he came to his knees in front of her, mirroring her very pose of a few minutes ago.

The look in his eyes made her insides ache even though she wasn't sure what it was. So Anya went on the defensive. "Before you ask, yes, I'm definitely going to have the baby."

"Okay."

"And I'm not going to hide it from anyone—not the

industry, not the media, not Meera. I'm not going to treat my pregnancy or my child as if it was some kind of bizarre mistake or sordid secret. I want this baby. Very much so."

"Okay."

"And I need your help in figuring out how we're… going to break the news to Meera that we won't be getting married. I mean, I understand that it might…make her feel insecure after everything she's been through, but I can't marry you. Not even to give this baby legitimacy."

"Okay," he agreed readily.

Perversely, his not insisting that they should marry made her want to cry. God, she was a contrary mess right now.

"So I guess your proposal is finally off the table then?" he asked with such mock seriousness that Anya wanted to kick him in that hard stomach.

"Yes."

"Other than those important announcements you just gave like a bloody queen, you're good? Your anxiety, your…tiredness?"

"Yes. I don't have nausea, or morning sickness or anything. My doctor already put me on the lowest dosage of anxiety medication for a while now and she said it won't cause any harm to the baby. I'm perfectly healthy—mostly hungry and horny, actually. Like all the time."

His mouth twitched and Anya felt as if she'd won a grand prize. One blunt-nailed finger traced her knuckles, up and down, side to side. A great, shuddering sigh left him. "I've dug us an even bigger pit to crawl out of, haven't I?"

"Well, it took two of us and a wall to make this baby, so it's a bit arrogant to think it's all on you."

"It was our first time then?"

"By my calculations, yes. I guess I should have told you that that condom in my bag was a few years old. I… I just wanted you…needed you so much that night that I didn't even think it might be out of date."

This time, the corner of his mouth quirked up in that crooked smile of his that she adored so much. "I needed you too."

He pushed a slightly shaky hand through his hair before looking up at her again. "Will you listen to me if I tell you what happened between Rani and me?" Before she could say either way, he pressed a hand to her mouth. "I want to tell you because I want you to know. To see why it took me so long to realize what I have in you. To realize what a blessing you are to me.

"Because you were absolutely right. I was using everything that happened with Rani as a grand reason to not move forward in life. I was letting guilt corrode everything. Letting fear control me. To not admit, even to myself, how hopelessly in love I was with you."

Her lower lip trembled, hot liquid rushing to her eyes as if there was a geyser waiting to erupt behind them. "Simon…you don't have to…"

"Although you have to give me some allowance for not seeing the truth when it was staring me in the face, Anya. I haven't been in love for so long, not since I first met Rani over two decades ago. I'm rusty as hell and

Rani's death took away my trust in myself. That's the worst part. I lost myself—my dreams, my desires, my joy for life. When we met, I was simply going through the motions for Meera's sake. Even she could see that."

Anya understood exactly what he meant about losing faith in oneself.

Her silence however made him draw in a deep breath. "Have I ever lied to you, Angel?"

Anya took a deep, shuddering breath. "No."

Simon pushed to his feet and wrapped his arms around her. "Shh...sweetheart. No more tears, please. I can't bear to see it." But more than his words, the scent of him was like a kick to her heart. Everything within her settled.

Anya patted the space next to her on the bed. While her feet dangled, his legs kicked into a long sprawl. While they weren't looking at each other, she smiled as Simon took her hand and laced their fingers together. As if he didn't want their connection to be lost even for a second.

"Meera coming into our lives at the time she did... was a saving grace. Not just for our marriage, but for Rani. She'd already been through a lot trying to conceive. We'd been married for a decade and our marriage was at its weakest. Her career—even though she was at the top—had already lost some of its allure for her. Rani, you see," he added with a long sigh, "used to thrive on challenge, on new things to be conquered, on being needed and adored. It took me a long time to see that about her."

Anya waited, knowing that this was hard for him.

"So when Meera came, it was as if Rani got a new lease on life. She wrapped up projects she couldn't get out of, got her lawyer to break contracts on a couple and threw herself into motherhood. But when Meera turned ten, things started changing. Rani raised her to be strong and independent and that's exactly how Meera turned out. But Rani...grew restless then, started saying Meera didn't need her as much anymore. I was traveling a lot and I didn't take her seriously."

He turned to face her then, and the ache in his eyes made Anya's chest ache. "It's not that she didn't love Meera or being a mother."

Anya shook her head. "You don't have to clarify that, Simon. You really don't. Some women are happy with just being mothers. Some need more challenges. There's no wrong or right."

Simon nodded. "Rani had those low periods before. She'd complain about being in a rut, that she needed a new hobby, that her body and her brain were vegetating. When I realized it continued to bother her, I reminded her that it had been her dream once to start an acting school. We went to dinner that night, just the two of us. She was glowing when she said she knew what she wanted. What would give her a new lease on life again."

"Another baby?" Anya whispered.

"Yes." He rubbed a hand over his face, his mouth tight and pinched. "To say that I was shocked would be an understatement."

"Did you argue?"

"Not that day, no. I thought she'd listen to reason.

I told her we should be glad that Meera was ten now. Tried to remind her that we'd been waiting for her to grow up so that they could both travel more with me. That there was no way, even if we could conceive by some miracle, that either of us wanted to go through the nappies-and-formula stage again. She seemed to agree with me and with usual masculine obliviousness—" his voice rang with bitterness "—I thought that was that."

Anya tightened her grip on his fingers and leaned her body against his to remind him she was there. That she was listening.

"A month later, she told me she'd made an appointment with a new fertility expert. I refused to even indulge in the idea of IVF again. I didn't want any more children and I definitely didn't want them at the cost of Rani putting her mind and body through all those hormone shots and pain again when it didn't work when we were younger. She retreated from me after that argument. For months and months, all I got from her was silence. It corroded everything good between us, killed what little we still had in common. She wouldn't talk or engage, only wanted a yes from me. And the damned good actress she was, she made it look like nothing was wrong in front of Meera."

He looked at his hands, as if he couldn't bear to hold Anya's gaze. As if he still felt shame over his actions. Anya's heart ached.

"I thought she'd get over it in the end, see reason. I was busy launching a new hotel in Seychelles and I was traveling a lot. I even asked her if she and Meera would like to join me. She said she had plans with some old friends in Mumbai. She sounded so excited that I thought she was through the low. That she was finding her feet again. I was so happy that we'd made it to the other side of this rough patch too." A shuddering sigh left him. "I was a damned fool. She took Meera with her to Mumbai. When I came back from Seychelles, she told me she'd signed on to the movie project and that must be when she visited a divorce lawyer too. She told me if I didn't give her what she needed in our marriage, she could at least revive her career. As if I had ever stopped her before."

"What happened?"

"I got mad…not because she wanted to go back to acting. But that she was so adamant about trying to conceive that she was giving me no choice at all. That she held that as some kind of sword over my head to prove that I still loved her, that I wanted the marriage. We got into a huge argument. She was furious with me and drove off. Her car totaled an hour later and she died. I don't even know where she was going. The last thing she heard from me was an accusation that she had destroyed our whole marriage and everything I had ever felt for her." A broken smile curved his mouth.

"I'm so sorry, Simon. Those words must have haunted you."

"They have, ever since she died. I don't want to paint her as some kind of villain, Angel. Because she wasn't. She adored Meera."

Anya searched for the right words, knowing that there might not be any. "I would never think that of her.

No one who knows Meera's confidence, Meera's faith in the mere memory of her mother, would think that."

"One minute we were arguing, the next she was gone. I started seeing myself as a monster. I was the one who'd denied her what she so desperately wanted. I was the one who'd blindly decided we'd ride it out if I just ignored her demands. If I had agreed to the IVF, maybe she'd have conceived this time. Maybe it wouldn't have pushed her into that restlessness again. Maybe she wouldn't have been driving so recklessly that day. Maybe she wouldn't have felt so alone. The truth was, we didn't love each other anymore. Guilt ravaged me after her death, not grief, and that realization made it even worse, like a vicious cycle."

"You can't just assume that she was driving recklessly, Simon. It could simply have been a ghastly accident. You can't go down that way of thinking—it'll end up destroying you."

"How can I not, Anya?"

"Because you yourself told me how much she loved Meera. I've seen that love in every word Meera speaks. You know, in your heart, Simon, that Rani would have never endangered her life like that. Not when she knew how it might affect Meera." Anya took his hands, willing him to see her. "You have to remember that she loved Meera. That while your marriage might have been irretrievably broken, she wasn't, Simon. You have to remember her as a capable, brilliant woman. The woman you once admired and respected and loved. Just because things fell apart between you two doesn't mean her verve for life was over."

"I do, now." Sadness lingered in his eyes but there was also acceptance. "It took me all this time to see that. That guilt will make you see horrible things, corrupt everything that's good and right too. That Rani lived a full, wonderful life that got cut short brutally. I know she would have thrived whatever new direction life took her in. It just wouldn't have been as my wife."

He pulled her up and into his lap before Anya could draw another breath. "Something Virat said at your birthday party made me take stock of the fear I was clinging to in the name of guilt. And sweetheart, I've been so in awe of you…and how bravely you've reached for life, how full of love and generosity and courage you are. How you decided that you'd just love Meera whether she knew who you were or not. How you made me come alive. Made me see I was denying myself happiness because of useless guilt. God, if Rani were here, even she'd have told me I'd become a foolish old man. That I was lucky to have another chance at love."

Anya hid her face in his throat. "I'm sorry for being so disrespectful toward her memory by saying I resented her. I was just miserable that you seemed to be leaving me when I was in love with you, and I know now that my body was also putting me through a hormonal wringer… I was at my worst. I'm sorry, Simon."

"Hush, sweetheart. The Rani I once knew would've never asked me to live a false life, bound to her. Not when my heart wasn't in it anymore. You're the most real thing I've ever seen, Angel, even when you think you're at your worst."

"You've made it easy for me to be brave, Simon. You make it so…easy to love you. You gave me everything I needed before I even knew I needed it."

"Then is it that hard to believe I feel the same about you, Anya?" His mouth peppered soft, butterfly kisses over her eyes, her nose, her cheeks and then the corner of her mouth. "I'm so absolutely in love with you, Angel." His palm moved to her belly and Anya felt his shuddering gasp as he felt the small but distinct swell of her belly. "And this baby…"

She shook her head, feeling as if she was being cleaved in two. "Please, don't lie to me, Simon. I can take anything but lies. You never wanted another child. You've said that enough times. I know you'd never resent an innocent child but he or she deserves more. I deserve more."

"You do," he said, rubbing the lone tear on her cheek. "Absolutely. You and this baby deserve to be loved and cherished. And I'd never lie to you. But will you hear the truth in my words? Will you give me that much, Angel?"

Anya nodded, every cell in her wanting him, wanting a future with him.

His gaze was steady, full of faith in her, full of love and affection that was like a balm to her soul. "Our marriage was already damaged even before Rani decided having a child would fix her. Would fix us. I couldn't imagine bringing a baby into that kind of unstable atmosphere. But you…you came into my life when I never expected to have another chance at love. I had all but given up on myself. I never expected to fall so madly in love with you, Anya. I fought it every inch. But God, now, I can't imagine life without you by my side. Can I not feel the same about this baby? How could I not fall in love with an innocent child that's a part of you and me? How could I not want a future with you and this baby and Meera, as a family?"

"I'd hate for you to resent me. For you to feel caught up in this without having had a say."

His fingers banding around the nape of her neck, he tilted her until she looked at him. "If you don't want to marry me, that's fine. I'm not at all worried about Meera because she knows how much I adore you. I don't care what the world or your brothers think. I only want you to know that I'm more than happy if you'll just let me be a part of your life and this baby's." He took her hand and kissed the knuckles, his gaze full of love. "All I want is a host of tomorrows with you, Anya."

Anya pulled her hand away and swatted his arm.

He froze, his heart in his eyes. How had she not seen it before? "Tell me what you need, Angel. Anything you want," he murmured, repeating the words he'd said to her that first evening.

Anya buried her fingers in his thick hair and tugged. "I mean, yes, I'm a modern woman but still… For once, Simon De Acosta, I want to be asked. I want to be cajoled. I want to be…persuaded into being your wife."

He was on his knees in a heartbeat and Anya laughed. In his big broad palm was the exact replica of a stunning ring they'd seen in his friend's collection which Anya had fallen in love with.

A giant ruby nestled among tiny diamonds and the whole thing was set in antique gold...a king's symbol of love for the girl he'd adored his entire life. "That's so beautiful. When did you have it made?"

"I saw how your eyes popped that night when Malik let us see his collection. I asked him if I could borrow it to get a replica made and he agreed. On the condition that we don't advertise where we got the design from. I was happy to reassure him that you would absolutely respect his need to keep the collection and all its valuable designs private."

"Oh...but that was weeks ago and you didn't even... know you were in love with me then."

Raising a brow, Simon made a mock bow. "Glad to know you have the timeline right in your head, Angel."

"Why did you have it made then?"

"Because even when I didn't understand it, or admit it, in my heart, I knew you were precious to me. I wanted to gift it to you because I knew how much you'd appreciate it. How much you'd adore it. And I wanted to make you happy. I wanted to give something to the girl who was strong and beautiful and as precious as this design."

Anya fell to the floor in an awkward movement, laughing and crying. Simon caught her, his arms tight around her, his embrace warm and everything she'd ever asked for. "You did give me something. My own heart back to me so that I could start living again. And it's now yours, to keep. I love you, Simon."

His mouth pressed to her temple, he dangled the ring in front of her. "I was also hoping that the ring might convince you, if my meager heart couldn't. I told myself that at least the artist in you might be tempted."

She swatted him and whispered against his mouth. "You still haven't asked me."

He took her mouth in a hard, demanding kiss that left her panting before he whispered, "Anya Raawal, will you marry me and put me out of my lonely misery? Will you and this baby be mine forever and ever? Will you give me a chance to make a family with you and Meera and this baby that I promise to love and cherish for the rest of my life?"

Anya looked into his steady brown eyes and said, "Yes."

He slid the ring onto her finger, his grin wicked and bright. And then he picked her up, closed the door to her bedroom, bolted it and then threw her on the bed, gently. And then he was covering her body with his and kissing her as if he couldn't last another second without it, and her legs fell apart to form a cradle for him and he was so hard and perfect against her core that Anya moaned into his mouth.

"Is this okay?" he asked, even though he hadn't let all his weight fall onto her.

Anya tugged at his hair and rubbed her cheek against his rough one. "It's perfect. And I missed you too. I missed this."

"You said you were horny, and I take my duties as your fiancé very seriously so we're going to find you relief and release very soon."

Anya giggled and he kissed her again, his eyes dancing with unholy delight. He continued kissing her while one busy hand gathered the hem of her long dress and his fingers were delving into her folds and Anya arched into his touch with a greediness she knew was never going to abate. "I hate to rush you, sweetheart, but since you're ready for me— Damn it, you are *so* ready for me," he mumbled the words into her neck. "I have a feeling the entire world is going to descend on us shortly and I'd love to give us both a release before they're all here."

Anya's shock turned into a raw moan when he thrust one finger into her and sensation pooled in her belly. "Who's coming?"

"You are," he whispered, licking at her pebbled nipple through the cotton of her dress.

Anya arched into his warm mouth before she pulled back. "I meant who's descending on us as you very well know, you beast."

He pushed her T-shirt out of his way, dragged his teeth over her plump, oversensitive nipple oh so gently, cursed at how her body greedily clutched his finger inside her and then he answered with a lazy grin. "Meera and your brothers and their wives and their children. And, oh, maybe your parents too."

"Oh, God. Hurry, please," Anya said, her climax already flickering so, so close.

Anya busied her hands with his trousers, and then he was inside her and her world felt right. Balancing his weight on his elbows, Simon thrust into her slow and deep, hitting her in exactly the right spot with such devilish intent that Anya thought she might die of the fast, rushing pleasure.

Lacing his fingers with her, Simon kissed the valley between her breasts, each swivel of his hips pushing her higher and higher. But it was his words, whispered warmly into her skin that flung Anya out of her own body. "I think I fell in love with you the first time you came for me."

Anya opened her eyes and held his gaze as his climax followed and she didn't stop whispering his name for a long time.

Just as Simon gathered her to him in a lazy cuddle, her phone pinged. They turned their heads together to see it was the astrology app telling her she was going to find love and she laughed and Simon laughed, and Anya thought that maybe the universe had finally gotten it right.

EPILOGUE

Eighteen months later

ANYA HAD FINALLY put her infant son, Rahul, down for a nap and stepped out into the main sitting lounge in the house Simon had built for them—close to her brothers' residences—only to find father and daughter shouting at each other.

"If either of you wakes that fussy son of mine with your argument, I swear I'm walking out the door and never returning. Then you two can fend for yourself and that cranky little guy. And the entire family that's descending on us in exactly…two hours."

Argument halted mid-words, Simon and Meera jerked their heads toward her, a guilty flush creeping up both their cheeks.

"Dad's saying I can't go to the party tonight, even though you both agreed I could like a month ago, and I promised to be back by ten."

Anya sighed, searching for the words where she didn't cut Simon's authority in front of Meera but also knowing that the girl was right. It didn't help that in the last eighteen months, Meera had lost all awkwardness and blossomed into such an achingly beautiful girl that Simon went a little berserk at the thought of the gangly teenage boys that surrounded her wherever she went.

Even now, as she stared at the teenager's stunning beauty, Anya's heart beat rapidly. Thank God they'd told Meera that she was her birth mother a few months after Rahul had been born.

Meera had listened to all of Anya's recounting of the past with a mature patience that had tugged at her. Her strong, fierce daughter had cried at first, had retreated for a few hours, even from Simon. That she'd gone into her baby brother's nursery and held him, which had made Anya cry even harder than Meera. After what had felt like an eternity and yet was only an hour, Meera had emerged brighter and braver if that was possible.

With fat tears in those wide eyes, she'd asked Anya if she'd be hurt if she didn't call her Mama. Because she'd wanted to reserve that for the woman who had raised her.

Anya had promised faithfully she'd never try to take Rani's place.

So they'd settled simply on Anya. Because that's what Meera was used to.

Not for a second did Anya begrudge Rani her place in Meera's memories or in her heart. And through it all, Simon had been there—patient, kind, loving, holding space for both Anya and Meera and then baby Rahul in his heart. Keeping every promise he'd ever made to cherish her, to cherish their family.

Of course, whatever small awkwardness Meera might have felt in her new relationship with Anya had been obliterated once she'd realized Vikram and Virat were really her uncles, that Zara and Naina were her aunts and that she had two little cousins to adore. Not that it had been completely smooth sailing.

Learning that the two most powerful men in Bollywood, two men she'd had a crush on for months, were her uncles had blown the teenager's mind and she was forever hanging around them.

Until she'd learned that they'd only been keeping their distance from her because of her dad's dictates that they give her time. Until she'd seen firsthand how overprotective those two uncles could get over their niece, given a half inch.

It had sent her beautiful daughter running screaming back into Anya's and Simon's arms, more than appreciative of her own parents, who believed in boundaries and open communication and treating her like an adult. Even her parents, Anya knew, had already lost a piece of their heart to this young woman who brought laughter and joy wherever she went.

For the first time in forever, her family had come together to protect Meera. They'd all rallied around her when it had been time to break the news to the media so that they could control the story. The promos of her first movie had begun to hit the press and eighteen months had changed her daughter a lot. Especially since with her tall, athletic build and distinctively strong features, Meera had begun to look more and more like Anya's mother.

Simon's stalwart support and her own innate confidence had helped Meera swim through that too.

Now, Meera adored her extended family—particularly her aunts and her little cousins, Zayn, Virat and Zara's son; Raima, Vikram and Naina's daughter; and her own little brother, Rahul. Especially since sometimes the little ones kept everyone's attention away from her own escapades.

"Anya, sweetheart, what is it?" Simon said, enfolding her in his embrace from behind, pulling her back into the present.

Even Meera stared at her, concern in her eyes. "Anya... I'm sorry I yelled at Dad. Are you okay?"

"I'm fine," Anya said, forcing a smile to her lips. Turning, she kissed Simon to the background noise of her teenage daughter making barfing sounds. When Simon watched her with concerned eyes, she smiled. "I'm just...so happy, Simon. So much has happened and sometimes the sheer joy catches me unawares."

Dropping his forehead to hers, Simon kissed her again. But this time, slowly, lazily, pouring everything he felt into the kiss.

"Anya, you have to talk to him about letting me go to the party. You're the only he'll listen to," Meera interrupted.

Simon and she laughed amid their kiss.

"We did agree to let her go, Simon," Anya said, patting the broad chest that had been her haven from the first moment they'd met. "And before you blame past us for making that decision, Vikram promised to keep an eye on her, remember? The party's being thrown by his friend's nephew."

"Ugh… Vikram uncle's going to be at the party? He's so much worse than Dad," muttered Meera. "I can't wait until Raima grows up and he's off my back. Although poor Raima deserves better than her over-protective dad hovering over her every minute."

"See, now your dad isn't looking so bad, is he?" Simon said, forever trying to pit himself favorably against Vikram.

"A little better. Very little," Meera finally relented with a small smile.

Anya raised a brow and suppressed a smile. "So you want to stay home and catch a movie with us then?"

"God, no. I don't want to see you two making cow eyes at each other."

"Hey!"

"What? Dad only returned from his trip yesterday. That's all you guys do anytime he's back. Why do you think I was so determined to go to this party in the first place?"

Anya burst out laughing. "Go then, before he changes his mind."

Despite all the attitude she gave them, Meera made a point to kiss Anya's cheek. Then she went up the stairs even though she was already dressed in ripped jeans and a crop top.

"Where's she going?" Simon asked, frowning. "Is she staying home? Did I win?"

Anya shook her head. "No, she never goes anywhere without kissing Rahul first."

Anya stayed in Simon's arms as Meera came back down, reluctantly kissed her dad's cheek and left out the front door. "We're going to the premiere tomorrow. Are you nervous?"

Meera stilled and bit her lip. "I am, yes. Terrified to be honest. But Virat uncle said it's one of his best and Vikram uncle said that's saying something because everything Virat uncle makes is brilliant and they both said… I did a good job."

Simon squeezed her shoulder. "You trust their judgment, right?"

"I do," Meera said, nuzzling her head into her dad's chest. One of those very rare happenings now that she'd just turned fifteen. She wrapped her arm around his waist and then turned a hesitant gaze up at Anya. "But even if I didn't…even if I sucked, that's okay, right?"

Anya opened her arms and Meera flew into them. "Is that why you've been acting extra-cranky around here lately?"

Meera's muffled "Maybe" made her laugh.

Simon wrapped his own arms around both of them, ignoring Meera's fake protest. "I'm sure you were brilliant, Meera. But even if you weren't, even if this is your first or last movie, it doesn't matter to us. We'll love you, support you in everything you do."

Sniffling, but refusing to show her face, Meera ran out of the living room.

The moment the door closed behind her, Simon lifted Anya in his arms and settled into a recliner with her on his lap. His fingers played with the hem of her shirt while he buried his mouth in her neck.

Anya arched into his caresses, nowhere near satisfied even after all these months. In fact, after giving birth to Rahul and the long hours with a newborn, all she wanted now was to spend every waking minute kissing and making love with Simon.

"You watched the movie already, didn't you?"

Anya tried to lie but she'd never been the actress in the family. It was her daughter who'd caught the gene. "Yes. I thought I should be prepared a bit."

"And?" Simon asked, arching a brow. While he'd made peace with the fact that her family was Bollywood royalty, as was Meera's mother, he was still the same protective dad she'd met on day one.

Anya laughed, then covered her mouth. "She's brilliant, Simon. I mean I knew it because Virat doesn't lie. She even outshines Zara...and that's saying something."

Simon groaned dramatically and Anya nipped his lower lip in retaliation. Lacing her fingers through his, he kissed each knuckle. "I wish I could say I'm surprised."

"We'll be there with her every step of the way, Simon," she said. In this matter, she was always the one who gave the reassurance.

"I know. And now that we have a teenager-free house, how long before your family descends on us again?"

"Hey... I guess I should tell Zara then that she shouldn't take Rahul along with them for the night, as we planned."

His eyes glittered with desire that was never far away. "I missed you."

Clasping his face, Anya kissed him sweet and deep and long. "I missed you too. And I want a full night with you, with no interruptions from our teething son."

"But let's not waste the two hours we have now, Angel," he said, before lifting her and carrying her to their bedroom. Where he applied himself dedicatedly to proving his love to her very thoroughly.

Or at least for the forty-five minutes before their son woke up and demanded to be cuddled.

* * * * *

If you couldn't put
The Secret She Kept in Bollywood *down*
be sure to check out the
Born into Bollywood duet
Claiming His Bollywood Cinderella
The Surprise Bollywood Baby

And don't forget to dive into these other
Tara Pammi stories!

An Innocent to Tame the Italian
A Deal to Carry the Italian's Heir
The Flaw in His Marriage Plan
The Playboy's "I Do" Deal
Returning for His Unknown Son

Available now!

WE HOPE YOU ENJOYED
THIS BOOK FROM
H HARLEQUIN
PRESENTS

Escape to exotic locations where passion knows no bounds.

Welcome to the glamorous lives of royals and billionaires,
where passion knows no bounds. Be swept into a world
of luxury, wealth and exotic locations.

8 NEW BOOKS AVAILABLE EVERY MONTH!

#4017 A BABY TO TAME THE WOLFE
Passionately Ever After...
by Heidi Rice
Billionaire Jack Wolfe is ruthless, arrogant...yet so infuriatingly attractive that Katherine spends a scorching night with him! After their out-of-this-world encounter, she never expected his convenient proposal or her response, "I'm pregnant..."

#4018 STOLEN NIGHTS WITH THE KING
Passionately Ever After...
by Sharon Kendrick
King Corso's demand that innocent Rosie accompany him on an international royal tour can't be denied. Neither can their forbidden passion! They know it can only be temporary. But as time runs out, will their stolen nights be enough?

#4019 THE KISS SHE CLAIMED FROM THE GREEK
Passionately Ever After...
by Abby Green
One kiss. That's all innocent Sofie intends to steal from the gorgeous sleeping stranger. But her moment of complete irrationality wakes billionaire Achilles up! And awakens in her a longing she's never experienced...

#4020 A SCANDAL MADE AT MIDNIGHT
Passionately Ever After...
by Kate Hewitt
CEO Alessandro's brand needs an image overhaul and he's found the perfect influencer to court. Only, it's her plain older stepsister, Liane, whom he can't stop thinking about! Risking the scandal of a sizzling fling may be worth it for a taste of the fairy tale...

HPCNMRA0522

#4021 CINDERELLA IN THE BILLIONAIRE'S CASTLE
Passionately Ever After...
by Clare Connelly

Tormented by the guilt of his past, superrich recluse Thirio has
deprived himself of the wild pleasures he once craved. Until
Lucinda makes it past the imposing, steel-reinforced doors of his
Alpine castle. And now he craves one forbidden night...with her!

#4022 THE PRINCESS HE MUST MARRY
Passionately Ever After...
by Jadesola James

Spare heir Prince Akil's plan is simple: conveniently wed Princess
Tobi, gain his inheritance and escape the prison of his royal life.
Then they'll go their separate ways. It's going well. Until he finds
himself indisputably attracted to his innocent new bride!

#4023 UNDONE BY HER ULTRA-RICH BOSS
Passionately Ever After...
by Lucy King

Exhausted after readying Duarte's Portuguese vineyard for an
event, high-end concierge Orla falls asleep between his luxurious
sheets. He's clearly unimpressed—but also so ridiculously sexy
that she knows the heat between them will be uncontainable...

#4024 HER SECRET ROYAL DILEMMA
Passionately Ever After...
by Chantelle Shaw

After Arielle saved Prince Eirik from drowning, their attraction was
instant! Now Arielle faces the ultimate dilemma: indulge in their
rare, irresistible connection, knowing her shocking past could taint
his royal future...or walk away?

**YOU CAN FIND MORE INFORMATION ON UPCOMING HARLEQUIN TITLES,
FREE EXCERPTS AND MORE AT HARLEQUIN.COM.**

HPCNMRB0522

*Tormented by the guilt of his past, superrich recluse
Thirio has deprived himself of the wild pleasures he
once craved. Until Lucinda makes it past the imposing,
steel-reinforced doors of his Alpine castle. And now he
craves one forbidden night...with her!*

*Read on for a sneak preview of
Clare Connelly's next story for Harlequin Presents*
Cinderella in the Billionaire's Castle.

"You cannot leave."

"Why not?"

"The storm will be here within minutes." As if nature
wanted to underscore his point, another bolt of lightning
split the sky in two; a crack of thunder followed. "You
won't make it down the mountain."

Lucinda's eyes slashed to the gates that led to the
castle, and beyond them, the narrow road that had brought
her here. Even in the sunshine of the morning, the drive
had been somewhat hair-raising. She didn't relish the
prospect of skiing her way back down to civilization.

She turned to look at him, but that was a mistake,
because his chest was at eye height, and she wanted to
stare and lose herself in the details she saw there, the
story behind his scar, the sculpted nature of his muscles.
Compelling was an understatement.

"So what do you suggest?" she asked carefully.

"There's only one option." The words were laced with displeasure. "You'll have to spend the night here."

"Spend the night," she repeated breathily. "Here. With you?"

"Not with me, no. But in my home, yes."

"I'm sure I'll be fine to drive."

"Will you?" Apparently, Thirio saw through her claim. "Then go ahead." He took a step backward, yet his eyes remained on her face, and for some reason, it almost felt to Lucinda as though he were touching her.

Rain began to fall, icy and hard. Lucinda shivered.

"I— You're right," she conceded after a beat. "Are you sure it's no trouble?"

"I didn't say that."

"Maybe the storm will clear quickly."

"Perhaps by morning."

"Perhaps?"

"Who knows."

The prospect of being marooned in this incredible castle with this man for any longer than one night loomed before her. Anticipation hummed in her veins.

Don't miss
Cinderella in the Billionaire's Castle,
available July 2022 wherever
Harlequin Presents books and ebooks are sold.

Harlequin.com

Get 4 FREE REWARDS!

We'll send you 2 FREE Books plus 2 FREE Mystery Gifts.

FREE Value Over **$20**

Both the **Harlequin® Desire** and **Harlequin Presents®** series feature compelling novels filled with passion, sensuality and intriguing scandals.

YES! Please send me 2 FREE novels from the Harlequin Desire or Harlequin Presents series and my 2 FREE gifts (gifts are worth about $10 retail). After receiving them, if I don't wish to receive any more books, I can return the shipping statement marked "cancel." If I don't cancel, I will receive 6 brand-new Harlequin Presents Larger-Print books every month and be billed just $5.80 each in the U.S. or $5.99 each in Canada, a savings of at least 11% off the cover price or 6 Harlequin Desire books every month and be billed just $4.55 each in the U.S. or $5.24 each in Canada, a savings of at least 13% off the cover price. It's quite a bargain! Shipping and handling is just 50¢ per book in the U.S. and $1.25 per book in Canada.* I understand that accepting the 2 free books and gifts places me under no obligation to buy anything. I can always return a shipment and cancel at any time. The free books and gifts are mine to keep no matter what I decide.

Choose one: ☐ **Harlequin Desire**
(225/326 HDN GNND)

☐ **Harlequin Presents Larger-Print**
(176/376 HDN GNWY)

Name (please print)

Address   Apt. #

City   State/Province   Zip/Postal Code

Email: Please check this box ☐ if you would like to receive newsletters and promotional emails from Harlequin Enterprises ULC and its affiliates. You can unsubscribe anytime.

Mail to the **Harlequin Reader Service:**
IN U.S.A.: P.O. Box 1341, Buffalo, NY 14240-8531
IN CANADA: P.O. Box 603, Fort Erie, Ontario L2A 5X3

Want to try 2 free books from another series! Call 1-800-873-8635 or visit www.ReaderService.com.

*Terms and prices subject to change without notice. Prices do not include sales taxes, which will be charged (if applicable) based on your state or country of residence. Canadian residents will be charged applicable taxes. Offer not valid in Quebec. This offer is limited to one order per household. Books received may not be as shown. Not valid for current subscribers to the Harlequin Presents or Harlequin Desire series. All orders subject to approval. Credit or debit balances in a customer's account(s) may be offset by any other outstanding balance owed by or to the customer. Please allow 4 to 6 weeks for delivery. Offer available while quantities last.

Your Privacy—Your information is being collected by Harlequin Enterprises ULC, operating as Harlequin Reader Service. For a complete summary of the information we collect, how we use this information and to whom it is disclosed, please visit our privacy notice located at corporate.harlequin.com/privacy-notice. From time to time we may also exchange your personal information with reputable third parties. If you wish to opt out of this sharing of your personal information, please visit readerservice.com/consumerchoice or call 1-800-873-8635. **Notice to California Residents**—Under California law, you have specific rights to control and access your data. For more information on these rights and how to exercise them, visit corporate.harlequin.com/california-privacy.

HDHP22